---- ★ ----

Ellie managed to sit up and push herself back from the body, her head churning with pain and confusion from trying to take in everything: the bump on her head, the cut on her temple, the growing darkness and cold, the approaching storm, and the dead body hidden under the leaves.

She was in the middle of the woods, injured, a storm on the way, alone except for Buddy, a dead body, and maybe a murderer or a rogue bear. For certainly, someone or something killed this man.

---- ★ ----

Previously published Worldwide Mystery titles by
JOANNE CLAREY

RIDDLED TO DEATH
HUMMINGBIRD FALLS

THE
FALL
HUNT

JOANNE CLAREY

W⬤RLDWIDE ®

TORONTO • NEW YORK • LONDON
AMSTERDAM • PARIS • SYDNEY • HAMBURG
STOCKHOLM • ATHENS • TOKYO • MILAN
MADRID • WARSAW • BUDAPEST • AUCKLAND

Recycling programs
for this product may
not exist in your area.

THE FALL HUNT

A Worldwide Mystery/October 2009

First published by Alabaster Books.

ISBN-13: 978-0-373-26689-0

Printed in U.S.A.

ACKNOWLEDGMENTS

I give heartfelt thanks to the many people, too numerous to mention here, who contributed to the creation of *The Fall Hunt*. Your suggestions, support and insight enriched its presentation. Special thanks to The Triad Roundtable of Writers, Dixie Land, David Shaffer, Lynette Hampton, D. J. Joyner, Larry Jakubsen, John Staples, James Isley and Helen Goodman; my readers and editors, especially Larry Jakubsen and Anne Garland; my book and cover designer, David Shaffer; and my family and friends, who guide, love and encourage me.

That night was the turning point in the season. We had gone to bed in summer, and we awoke in autumn; for summer passes into autumn in some unimaginable point of time, like the turning of a leaf.
—Henry David Thoreau

A change in the weather is sufficient to recreate the world and ourselves.
—Marcel Proust

When a man murders a tiger, it's called sport; when the tiger wants to murder him, it's called ferocity.
—George Bernard Shaw

ONE

Early September:

TROUBLE WAS THE LAST thing on Ellie's mind as she pushed open the Greenberg Federal Bank front door. For the last twenty minutes, she had enjoyed the scenic drive downhill from her cabin located in the tiny mountain village of Hummingbird Falls, to the city of Greenberg. Her beloved mutt, Buddy, whom she had rescued at the village dump last year, accompanied her as usual.

Greenberg was the closest place to bank, shop for groceries, and visit movie theatres, pharmacies, fast-food eateries, or malls. Hummingbird Falls offered none of these amenities, choosing instead to remain a quiet township of eight hundred residents, which drew tourists year-round because of its famous Hummingbird Falls, extensive cross-country ski trails and well-maintained hiking trails. It catered to the visitors with art galleries, inns, intimate resorts and golf courses, choice restaurants, and small antique and gift shops.

As Ellie and Buddy rode the back roads to Greenberg, delicious warm September air swept through the Subaru's open windows, blowing Ellie's short grayish-brown hair and ruffling Buddy's black-and-white fur. As usual, Ellie conversed with Buddy, who listened to every word and occasionally replied with a bark or a lick.

"We're almost there, Buddy. And I haven't figured out yet what to get Allison. She's turning twenty-five next week. It's hard to believe my baby's so old. It's harder to believe I'm old enough to have a daughter who's in her mid-twenties," she exclaimed.

Buddy whined softly.

"Thanks for your sympathy, Bud, but the truth is we're all getting older. Face it."

Ellie glanced at her image in the rearview mirror.

"Do you think I should dye my hair?"

Buddy barked twice and then curled up on the seat.

"You're right. I have other things to think about now. Like, what should I buy for a twenty-five year old successful, urban market researcher who has everything already?"

Ellie spent the rest of the drive to Greenberg contemplating what gift would be just right for Allison. She just about decided a gift certificate for a day at Allison's favorite spa might be nice as she opened the Greenberg Federal Bank's door.

All thoughts flew out of her mind as a ski-masked individual, dressed in black from head to toe, grabbed her arms and pulled them behind her back.

"What are you doing?" she gasped.

"Shut up. Do what I tell you and you won't get hurt," a gruff voice commanded.

Strong arms pushed Ellie toward the tellers' counter and then forced her down on the floor.

"Lie down, face to the floor. Put your hands over your head and close your eyes."

Ellie did what the gruff voice told her without protesting. She had just enough time to see a group of people lying facedown in the lobby of the bank and several people all in black, clustered like crows behind the tellers' counter. Then someone put a cloth over her eyes, pulled it tight and tied it behind her head.

"What do you want?" Ellie asked. "You can have my purse. There's not much in it, I'm afraid."

"Shut up, lady. I mean it. Don't make me hurt you."

Ellie felt a shoe step down hard on her back. She squeezed her lips together as tightly as she could. She said a silent prayer rather than risk more danger by antagonizing the menacing crow with the many questions she ached to ask. Then the shoe lifted. Ellie forced herself to stay absolutely still. She held her breath, afraid any movement might cause a fatal reaction.

The cold marble floor chilled the skin on her face and arms, slowly ate its way through her clothes, and seemed to seep into her bones. She shivered. Fear threatened to overcome her as she acknowledged the gravity of the situation she faced.

TWO

MOMENTS LATER, she heard footsteps walking away from her. She strained to hear other sounds. Faint whispering came from the direction of the tellers' counter. She heard muffled sobs; a woman was crying nearby. A loud cough suddenly hacked through the quiet, startling her heart into overdrive. Ellie's heart pounded so fast and loud, she feared the robbers would think she was drumming a cry for help. Then what would happen? She willed herself to breathe slowly and calm down.

When no one else threatened her or the other hostages, Ellie's racing heart began to slow. Rational thought returned to her little by little. Her brain started to function again and with it, her curiosity. She wanted to see what was happening. How many robbers were there? Where were they? How could she escape?

The first obstacle she faced was the blindfold. She needed to move it enough so she could see, but not so much the robbers would notice. Using her hands was out of the question; one of the robbers must be watching the group on the floor.

A memory jumped into Ellie's mind. She recalled the drama clearly, as she watched the movie play in her head. She was at her best friend Susie's ninth birthday party, playing pin-the-tail on the donkey. Susie's mother blindfolded Billy Finn and spun him until he was dizzy. The children roared with laughter as Billy stumbled in the opposite direction from the donkey poster. Billy bent over, laughing too.

Ellie saw Billy nudge the blindfold up with his arm as he straightened. No one else seemed to notice. Then Billy turned around, walked to the poster and placed the tail precisely. Ellie was so stunned that he had cheated, she couldn't speak. Dishonesty of any kind was abhorrent to her, even at the age of nine. To make matters worse, Billy won first prize. His cheating, and being rewarded instead of punished, violated her strict sense of justice.

Remembering how Billy manipulated his blindfold inspired Ellie. She moved her face against the cold marble floor, trying to push the blindfold up enough so she could see. The floor was too slick; the cloth found no resistance. It didn't move at all.

Disappointed but not defeated, Ellie tried several more times. The blindfold remained in place.

She'd have to try something else. She couldn't see, but maybe she could hear some information which would help her free herself and the others.

Along with the sobbing, the coughing and the whispering of several voices, she could distinguish the sound of rustling paper and the footsteps of more than a few people.

Those footsteps must be the robbers', Ellie thought. There's got to be at least four or five of them.

A yell sent Ellie's face back to the cold marble floor. "Shut up," the gruff voice shouted. "I can't stand your crying. If you don't stop, I'll give you something to cry about."

The sobbing woman went silent. Hoping to take advantage of the distraction, Ellie rubbed the blindfold against her arm. It shifted a little. She pushed at it again.

If she looked down as far as possible, she could see some light and a tiny slice of the floor. One or two more slight adjustments and she might be able to see enough to figure out what was happening. Very slowly, she moved the cloth once more across her arm and then lay still.

She could only see three or four feet downward and behind and not at all above her. However, if she twisted her head just a little in different directions her line of vision improved.

She counted five bodies, three men and two women, on the marble floor around her. She knew the crying woman was ahead of her, so that made six. The coughing man was seven. From her quick first glimpse before the robber blindfolded her, she knew four or five others were lying on the floor, now out of her line of vision. The bodies she could see were lying like her, on their stomachs, eyes blindfolded with white cloth, hands stretched over their heads in hopeful obedience.

Stretching her neck bit by bit as far as she could without being obvious, Ellie strained to see the tellers' area where she had heard the whispering. She counted three pairs of identical black athletic shoes below three pairs of black sweat pants standing in front of the counter. No matter how hard she tried, she couldn't see any higher.

She watched, looking for any clues as to what the bank robbers were doing, or who they might be. At times, if the angle was just right, one of the black-suited thieves would move into full view. Then Ellie could see a whole body. However, since each robber was masked and gloved, she couldn't identify skin color, let alone age, or sex. Could one of them be a woman? The best clue to identification Ellie had was height and weight. With their baggy outfits, they all looked pretty much the same weight to her. One robber was taller than the others were; one was shorter. Looking for clues for identity was like trying to distinguish one crow out of a flock.

Unexpectedly, Ellie remembered the old-fashioned term used to describe a group of crows. A murder of crows! She prayed these crow-like figures were not planning to murder their hostages. Ellie shivered away those thoughts and continued her investigation.

What were they doing, milling around? Why didn't they take the money and run? What were they waiting for? Ellie rested her neck muscles, laying her head back on the floor for a moment. When she looked up again, she didn't see any of the robbers. Had the flock flown?

Since the woman had stopped crying and the coughs were stifled, an eerie silence filled the bank.

No, Ellie thought. Not total silence. True, she couldn't hear any voices talking, but she could hear something. What was it? The bank robbers must have finished stuffing bags with money. So what was the faint noise she heard?

The sound grew louder. A car or truck had pulled up to the back of the bank. The robbers must be ready to escape.

Ellie marveled at how well the thieves orchestrated the robbery. Obviously, their plan succeeded without any problems. No inexperienced gang members or desperate-for-money drug addicts, these robbers were professional. They expressed no anxiety and used no personal names. They took their time, seemed to be working well together, and didn't harm the hostages, at least not yet. They chose matching costumes to make identification more difficult and prepared the blindfolds in advance. Now they were going to get away, out the back door, without a shot fired, or a voice raised against them.

She heard a quiet dinging, like a wristwatch's alarm would make. She twisted her head toward the noise. She saw several pairs of shoes walking in her direction. Ellie lowered her head and held still, hoping they hadn't noticed her blindfold was higher than before. She watched the feet move closer.

Then they were right next to her. She held her breath, staring at the shoes, praying they'd continue moving on, fearful they wouldn't. For a second her mind registered something wrong about the shoes, something strange. Then Ellie's terror snuffed out all thought and she squeezed her eyes shut.

The shoes didn't stop; they walked on past her, toward the back of the bank.

When Ellie dared look again, the robbers were out of sight. She heard a car door slam, a motor revving its engine, another set of slamming doors and a vehicle driving off fast.

Then nothing. Only silence.

THREE

Mid-September:

"BUT JAMES, I DON'T want to talk about how I felt. I just want to stop the nightmares, be able to walk back into the bank, and remember what I saw. I know I saw something important. Something that would help the police. It's driving me crazy."

Ellie turned from the window in James's office. She had been staring at the bright autumn colors without seeing them. She walked back to the chair facing James, plunked down, and sighed.

"Don't worry. The nightmares will stop. You'll go into the bank again. You'll remember what you forgot. You just have a touch of post-traumatic stress reaction, PTSR, which is perfectly normal after experiencing such a frightening event."

James got up and walked over the bookcase, stuffed with volumes. He pulled a few out, put them back and then found the one he was looking for. He walked back and sat down.

"Recovery can be fairly quick. But you've got to be patient and give yourself more time. It hasn't even been two weeks since the robbery. Of course you're still having some effects. I asked about your feelings because research indicates talking about what happened, the feelings you experienced, helps speed up the process."

"What helps me remember what I've forgotten?" Ellie picked at her cuticles while she stared intently at James.

"Well, some people try a hypnotist. Others write detailed chronological logs and hope recalling the event systematically will bring the blank moment back. Others get help from therapists. We treat the children with PTSR and PTSD here at Foster's Home for Children with a varied mix of modalities."

"Hmm. Does anyone succeed in putting the trauma to rest? Forgetting it and moving on?"

"Sure," James answered, smiling, as he handed Ellie the book he had selected. "All the time. Here, try this book. It does a good job of explaining what you're going through. The author makes some excellent suggestions on how to deal with PTSR."

"Thanks." Ellie studied the cover of the book and then turned it over and scanned the information on the backside. She looked at James.

"I admit, at times I feel now just as scared as I did that day. Especially when I'm alone, or hear a loud noise. I guess I haven't released all the fear. Sometimes I wake up in a sweat from dreams about being frozen to an icy floor and not being able to get up. I can't go in the bank, although I've tried a few times. I start to panic when I reach the door."

Ellie paused, remembering. Then she shook her head as if to dislodge the memory. "But the worst part, James, is obsessing over what I can't remember. My mind just won't let it go. I know I saw something, something so critical it could crack the case wide open. I just can't remember what it is. I feel so blocked."

Ellie brought a tissue to her eyes and dabbed at tears beginning to form. "Why can't I remember?"

"Sometimes what helps us remember is doing just what we think we shouldn't," James smiled at Ellie and patted her arm softly.

"Explain, please. I'm a bit thick today. Excuse the wet eyes. I don't normally get teary-eyed. Too old and tough for tears." Ellie tried to laugh, but the sound came out more like a mangled sob.

"Tough, yes. Old, no way. Anyway, everyone cries. Tears aren't a sign of weakness; they just help release stress and express feelings. After what you've been through, you deserve a good cry. And sometimes, tears make eyes shine more beautifully, like yours are right now."

Ellie blushed. The welling tears melted away.

"You sure know how to make a woman feel better. Thanks, James. I appreciate your helping me. I'm okay now, really. Finish what you were saying about how to remember something."

"Well, you tell yourself you're putting the problem away, letting your brain work on it while you do other things, normal routine activities. And then you just do it. Work outside, read a book, do the dishes. Many people come up with the name, date, place or memory in the middle of doing something else."

"I could try that, I suppose," Ellie said. "I certainly have many things I should be doing. I'll read the book you gave me, too."

She glanced at her watch. "Oh, I didn't know it was so late. I have to go and I'm sure you have lots to do. Thanks for your help and for fitting me in your busy schedule."

"Anytime, Ellie. If you want to talk, give me a call."

The two walked to James's office door.

James said, "Say, why don't we go to dinner on Thursday night? We can talk more about the robbery or what's still bothering you, if you want. However, I'd love to see you even if you'd rather talk about politics, football scores, the trouble with education, or just sit quietly with me and enjoy a good meal. It's been too long since we've spent some time alone."

Ellie turned and gave James a hug.

"I know. I've missed our dinners, too. I'd love to. Thursday's good."

As Ellie headed for her car, her smile faded, replaced by a frown. Once alone, her mind returned to its endless digging through the events of the bank robbery. Like a gardener turning over clay-hard soil, trying to loosen it and search for stones and roots, she probed deeply into her memory hoping to relax its resistance and find the hidden details. What did she see? What was blocking her? Why couldn't she remember?

Ellie had all questions and no answers. She felt compelled to find the answers. She worried her obsession might take control of her life if she didn't figure out what she saw soon. The idea of a mania this strong dominating her filled her with fear.

FOUR

Last Week of September:

ELLIE WOKE TO the cawing of crows. She yawned, stretched, and like a waking bear, unleashed a round of early-morning groans. She ambled toward the bathroom, passing the bedroom window on her way. She glanced out. What she saw in her backyard brought her to an abrupt standstill. She stood motionless, gaping. Her blue eyes, framed with wire-rimmed glasses, fixed on the scene outside her window.

Instead of maroon and yellow chrysanthemums, red sedum and purple asters blasting color against the evergreen of the rhododendrons, she saw chaos and ruin in the flowerbeds.

Ellie broke out of her daze and called for Buddy.

"Buddy, come on. Something terrible happened."

She ran to the back door and slipped her old green fleece jacket over her flannel nightgown. As an afterthought, she pulled on a bright orange wool cap and some matching orange gloves. Then she stepped into her high green Wellingtons and hurried out into the backyard with Buddy.

Early-morning sun sparkled miniature diamonds on the snow already dusting the tops of the highest mountains. Below the timberline and around Ellie's yard, the woods wore nature's palette: the ochre leaves of birches, the crimson of maples, the sienna of oaks, the burned-orange of ash, the rose of the elms and the purple of wild cherry trees. The conifers, fir, hemlock, spruce, cedar, pine and juniper added forest-greens and teal-blues.

Seven crows sat in the highest branches of the old oak tree. They watched Ellie and Buddy walk into the backyard. However, Ellie didn't notice them or nature's beauty this morning. She was focusing on the ghastly spectacle on the ground before her. Oblivious, Buddy romped around, etching abstract patterns on the frosted grass. Clouds of steam puffed from his mouth as he frolicked in the icy air.

The first hard frost of the season had sneaked in last night like a vampire, covering the grass in a silvery white shroud and decimating the gardens Ellie had toiled over throughout the spring and summer. The cold night stalker withered blooms and shrunk flowers to skeletal stalks, sucked their energy until they were pale and faded, then killed them. The invisible invader disappeared before dawn, leaving the bodies of his victims scattered helter-skelter on the cold ground.

"Oh, Buddy. Our first fall in our new cabin in Hummingbird Falls and already we've had two disasters. First, the awful experience at the Greenberg Bank and now the frost has killed every flower on our new perennials. Oh, dear."

She breathed out a huge puff of steamy air. "I worked so hard on these gardens. Now they're just a mess."

Ellie bent over and picked up a brown stalk topped with a withered, once-yellow chrysanthemum.

"Poor thing. I wasn't expecting this to happen. Everything's gone." Ellie dropped the dead flower on the ground. She looked out over the rest of the gardens.

"Buddy, I'm sad to say, the frost has come and destroyed the last of our flowers. Now, we'll have to bed down the gardens. I don't like these sudden changes. Makes me feel, I don't know, sort of out of control. Anything can happen anytime, when you least expect it."

Ellie had pulled up most of the annual flowers and vegetable plants weeks ago, but she'd have to cut back the dead brown stalks, scatter seed-holding pods, mulch the perennial beds and bury bulbs for next spring's bloom: daffodils, crocus, alliums, narcissi and iris.

"No more flowers for a while, Buddy. I'll miss them."

She and Buddy wandered through the gardens, inspecting the brown frost-killed perennial flowerbeds. She gazed across the lawn, pensive, a poem rising in her mind about the passing of summer and arrival of fall. The sudden death of her plants was symbolic of how quickly life can change. The theme of her poem would focus on how the sadness from such an unexpected loss can transform into happiness with time, just as her perennials would bloom again in the spring. New flowers would emerge from the bulbs she would bury in the dirt.

After all, didn't she survive the death of her husband, Chris, ten years ago? Back then, Ellie thought her life was over. The love for her two children was her main reason for continuing. Then with time, she found happiness again, here in Hummingbird Falls.

She decided to head back to the cabin to jot down her poetic thoughts when she saw the hummingbird feeder smashed on the ground. Like blood on a white sheet, sticky red liquid splattered across the frosted ground. The hummingbirds migrated weeks ago, so they wouldn't miss their sugar water, but she would have to replace the broken feeder next spring. Then she saw the other bird feeders, in pieces, pulled from the trees where they had provided mixed seeds and suet for the birds all spring and summer.

FIVE

"OH, BUDDY. OUR FEEDERS. They're ruined. What happened?

With a chorus of loud cawing, the seven crows took flight into the air, circled the backyard once, and then flew toward the thick forest, as if in pursuit of the vandal.

Ellie and Buddy ran over to the chaos of seeds, shattered glass, broken wood, and bent-up wire suet holders flung around the grass. Ellie surveyed the damage, holding on to Buddy's collar to keep him from stepping into the broken glass.

"Just look at this, Buddy. Was it those pesky squirrels? No. I don't believe they could do so much destruction. At most, they only gnaw and chew a little and occasionally knock a feeder down. Maybe it was those crows; some say they're harbingers of trouble. Well, something or someone ripped these feeders apart. We can't use any of them again."

Buddy looked up at Ellie, turning his head slightly at each inflection of her voice. He was giving his full attention to her monologue, which was all Ellie needed to continue her conversation.

"I'll tell you what I think. At first glance, and without in-depth study of the crime scene and careful analysis of the situation the way my dear Miss Marple would do,

I would guess the culprit's a mean-spirited person. Although I can't think of one person in Hummingbird Falls mean-spirited enough to do this.

"Hmm. Maybe someone's angry at me. But who? Did I annoy someone? I can't think of a soul who I've hurt or treated badly. I don't think anyone I fined for an overdue book would resort to this.

"But there has to be a motive. There's always a reason for everything, even if we don't know what it is. Surely, no one I know is starving enough to rip apart bird feeders for a little seed and suet.

"We'll get to the bottom of this mystery, Buddy. I'll report the damage to Dave and find out if others have had their feeders tampered with. I'm not putting up with vandals coming onto my property and causing havoc."

Looking down at Buddy, Ellie continued, "Can you help me, boy? Go sniff around. Try to smell someone or something. Maybe we'll find some footprints or evidence."

Buddy looked up at Ellie with a quizzical look. He answered her question by nosing toward the broken feeders and growling loudly. Then he barked.

"What is it, Buddy? Do you smell something? Go on. Follow the trail."

Ellie pulled Buddy away from the broken glass and then let go of his collar. With nose to ground, Buddy sniffed his way to the edge of the lawn and barked at the blueberry bushes. They banked the yard, holding back the mixed-wood forest behind.

Ellie followed Buddy, her eyes searching for footsteps in the frost. "Maybe if we spot a print we can make a casing, like they do on those forensic shows.

Then we can match the casing to the shoes of possible vandals and get Dave to talk to them."

But Ellie didn't see any footprints; the frost had covered over any evidence that a vandal might have left.

Buddy edged closer to the blueberry bushes. The high-bush blueberry leaves had turned fiery red and hid the space beneath them where red bunchberry and moss covered the ground. Ellie had long since stripped the blueberry bushes of their fruit. Most of blueberries rested within flaky-pastry pie shells in Ellie's freezer.

Buddy continued to growl and sniff and then lifted his leg and peed on the lower branches.

"You tell 'em, boy. Mark our territory. This's our land and we won't tolerate any riffraff invading and destroying our feeders, just when the birds need them the most."

After scrutinizing under the blueberry bushes and behind several other shrubs and finding nothing of consequence, Ellie called Buddy.

"Come on, boy. I don't think we'll find any clues here. Let's go in and eat our breakfast while I jot down a few ideas for my poem before I forget them. Then I'll get dressed, drive to the police station and tell Dave what happened.

"While we're in town we'll stop at the deli and buy some new feeders, suet and seed. Maybe Reggie has heard complaints about smashed feeders. Then we'll check at the Pastry Shop and see what the locals think. Everyone in there has something to say about everything."

Ellie turned and for a moment looked at her once lovely gardens. She noted the outdoor work she'd have to complete and sighed. "Oh, well, Buddy," she said as they neared the back door, "cleaning up this mess and getting the gardens prepared for winter might help me lose some of the weight I've gained eating those luscious blueberry pies. So, you see, there's a good side to everything."

SIX

October:

MOST OF THE LEAVES had already floated their way to the frozen ground and skeletal branches of the deciduous trees raked the grey skies. The hummingbirds, bluebirds, robins and other seasonal birds had long since migrated, leaving crows, chickadees, nuthatches, woodpeckers, blue jays, titmice and other hardy birds behind. A Halloween mood descended on Hummingbird Falls and the excitement of autumn activities in the mountains grabbed hold of Ellie and Buddy, too.

As James predicted, Ellie's bad dreams disappeared and she could now bank at the Greenberg Federal bank with no trepidations. She had conquered most of her fears and felt confident again. Only one problem continued to plague her.

She could not remember the important facts she had blocked out from that day. She remained obsessed with trying to burrow them out of her brain.

Ellie's haunting obsession had stiff competition, though. The exhilaration of traditional fall events enticed the residents of Hummingbird Falls, including Ellie. At her friends' urging, she joined in the fun.

Residents were busy creating scenes featuring people made from pumpkins. Pumpkin-people were pop-

ping up at farm stands, in front yards and at every inn
and restaurant in the village. Ellie and Buddy drove
around town and saw pumpkin-people picking pumpkin trees, raking lawns, fishing, playing soccer, skiing,
cuddling baby pumpkins, climbing pumpkin mountains, picking banjos and exhibiting every activity
imaginable. Many leaf-peeping tourists were following
the village map indicating where the pumpkin-people
were located and then driving back to the Chamber of
Commerce to cast their vote for the most creative dis-
play.

Ellie's new cabin sat so far back from the road, down
a long dirt driveway, she didn't bother to make her own
pumpkin-people creation. Instead, she worked with
volunteers at the library preparing a scene showing a
pumpkin librarian reading to a group of little pumpkin
children who looked enthralled.

Scents of apples, dry leaves, burning piles of yard
waste, steaming cider and hot-out-of-the-fat doughnuts
filled the chilly air. Everyone wanted to be outside,
bustling around the farmers' market, splitting wood or
stacking it, raking leaves, putting on storm windows,
driving orange-tipped stakes into the ground along
driveways to prepare for and alert the snow plows, or
walking the hills enjoying the view of the colorful
mountains topped with snow.

Ellie heard the sounds of chainsaws, hammers,
leaves rustling, mountain music jams, squeals of
excited children and the laughter of villagers echoing
off the mountainsides and bouncing back into the valley
as she worked preparing her garden for winter.

One warm Saturday Ellie left Buddy with Sarah,
and she, Bonnie and her three kids, and the Buckley

family—Todd, Millie, Matt, Missy and Mike—decided to tour the seven-acre corn maze.

They laughed at the warnings posted at the ticket sellers' table cautioning them to take the fifteen-minute maze first, testing their endurance and ability to challenge the labyrinth before attempting the super maze.

"We aren't going to do the baby maze, Dad, are we?" Matt asked. "We can do the big one. No problem."

Bonnie was a little more cautious. "My kids aren't as old as you, Matt. The big maze takes at least forty-five minutes to finish and it's hot today. Maybe we should split up. You guys go in the big one and we'll go in the shorter one."

"No," everybody protested, including Bonnie's kids.

"It'll be more fun if we're all together," Todd said. "It can't be too hard. If the little ones get tired, we'll carry them."

Ellie agreed. "If an older, slightly overweight woman like me dares to confront the mysteries of the labyrinth, they sure can. Look at all their energy."

Bonnie's kids were jumping up and down, dancing around, filled with the excitement of going into the colossal maze. "Come on, Mom. Let us go. We'll be fine. Please, please."

Bonnie laughed and said, "Okay, but remember you're the ones who begged to go. No whining later on."

The group picked up their clue lists and walked inside the maze. The corn towered six feet over them. The corn-maze designer had planted the corn so thick no one could possibly see or move through the rows. Signs warned everyone to stay on the paths mowed through out the maze.

"Whew, this's eerie," Missy said. "What do we do?"

"We just pick a path, choose which way we want to go and try to find station number one, which will give us a clue," said Ellie. The six kids went racing on ahead, screaming and laughing when they ended up at a dead end and had to turn back.

"Hurry up, you guys," they yelled as they disappeared down another path, passing several families who were backtracking. "Nothing down there," one of the parents called to Ellie's group. "Dead end."

"We're looking for number one," Bonnie called to their retreating backs.

"It's way back the way you came," they called back.

"Lost already and we haven't hit the first station," Ellie said. "Maybe this maze's tougher than we thought."

"Don't worry," said Millie. "We're really smart. We'll figure it out. Think of all those riddles you had to figure out last summer. You thought you'd been riddled to death. We'll work together on the maze like we did with those crazy clues you got."

After a while, the group dispersed. Bonnie lagged behind with her kids, who quickly tired and had had enough of the corn maze. They wanted an ice cream cone instead. Todd and Millie's children were nowhere in sight. The last time their parents saw them, they were running full speed, each trying to reach the next clue station first. Todd and Millie fell into a deep conversation and wandered wherever the paths led, paying more attention to each other than to the twists and turns of the maze.

Ellie found herself alone, at a dead end. She stared at the corn, reaching to the blue sky. Overhead, she saw a family of crows wheeling on the breeze. They reminded her of the robbers and she shivered, in spite of the heat. She looked around. No one else was in sight.

Sighing, she started back up the path and came to a cross path. Should she go left or right? She called out, "Millie, Bonnie, Todd. Anyone there?"

None of them answered. She must have strayed farther than she thought. She studied her choices. The left path stretched out and she could see many paths turning off it, left and right. She turned to the right.

Coming down the path was a man dressed all in black. He looked at her as he walked closer.

Ellie turned left and walked briskly. She looked over her shoulder. The man was following her. She ducked onto one of the side paths, praying that it wasn't a dead end, that it led to a clue station or to other people. She glanced back. The man had taken the same turn.

Then she ran out of path. It was another dead end. No way to turn. She tried forcing though the corn, but it was too thick and reinforced with an almost invisible wire fence. She had no choice. She turned and faced the man in black.

SEVEN

ELLIE'S MOUTH WAS DRY. She watched the man approach her, her hands formed into fists at her side.

The man stopped three feet in front of her. "Guess there's no way out from here."

Ellie stood there, her back to the corn, ready to fight this man with all the strength she could muster. Fear kicked her adrenaline up and she could feel drops of sweat wetting her shirt.

"Do you know where station ten is?"

Ellie shook her head no.

The man in black smiled. "This maze is harder than I thought. My kids are up on the tower in the middle yelling to me to hurry up. They pointed this way, I think, but obviously this isn't the right way."

Ellie shook her head no.

"Well, have fun," the man said as he started to turn back to the path.

Then he stopped and turned back. "Are you okay? You look a little flushed. Can I help? Do you want to walk along with me until you figure out where you are?"

Ellie shook her head no.

"Okay. Good luck. You'll probably make it out before I do," he said as he waved goodbye.

When Ellie saw the man turn right at the end of the

path and disappear, a wave of relief flowed over her. Her fists opened, her shoulders dropped and she lowered her head, resting her stiff neck. She stood quietly, trying to pull herself together.

A flurry of activity, a swarm of children, came barreling down the path to her. "Mrs. Hastings, Mrs. Hastings. Is this the way? Did you find station three yet?" Todd and Millie's kids dashed up to her. Before she could answer them, they answered themselves.

"No, stupid. Obviously, this's another dead end. Now we have to go all the way back again and take that other path, the one Matt said was wrong," Missy said.

"We're off, Mrs. Hastings. Follow us if you want. We're doing great, but we have to move fast. We want to beat our parents to the tower," said Michael. Then the three kids ran at breakneck speed up the path and turned left.

Ellie started to jog after them. She didn't want to walk alone in this maze again.

The group reunited, sweating, hot, thirsty and tired. Over an hour later, they finally found their way through all the numbered markers in the contorted and challenging labyrinth. As they climbed the tower located in the center of the maze, they realized they were only half-done. They now faced the daunting adventure of figuring their way back out through miles of intricate paths to the exit. No clue sheets helped visitors hunt out the exit's location. They stared over the maze and fixed their eyes on the exit flag.

"Just keep moving to the left and eventually we'll get out," Todd said.

The corn guides stationed on the tower spun tales of the folks who entered the maze and never made it out. These obviously fictional stories created laughter from the adults and stirred the kids up with new enthusiasm for facing the final part of the puzzling warren.

"Here we go again," Ellie sighed as the group trooped down the tower steps and into the maze once more. "Keep to your left, remember, and don't get all spread apart. We don't want to lose anybody."

After another frustrating hour, Ellie's group was too tired to go on. Even Matt gave up trying to escape the maze. They put in a call for a corn guide to help them out, much to their mortification. While they waited for the guide to find them, they talked about hunters and hikers who had become lost in the maze of the great forest.

Missy said, "I bet those lost people wished they had corn guides to help them."

"If Buddy were with us, I bet he could hunt out the exit," Ellie said, wishing Buddy had been with her when she faced the man in black.

Later, drinking their pumpkin smoothies and relaxing under the shade of a tent, all agreed. Even though they suffered humiliation because they called for help, the maze was spectacular and great fun.

The other huge event in October was the traditional haunting. Adult-oriented and filled with weird thrills, the tickets to the October haunting had almost sold out. When Ellie, Mike, James and his group of kids from the Foster's Home for Children arrived at the ticket booth, they learned the chilling adventure was so ghoulish the producers of the show, Death Dancers, Inc., wouldn't allow anyone under ten years old to participate. Fortunately, James knew about the age limit and the five kids he brought were all over twelve.

This year the famous Ghoulog haunting was taking place at Canton Mountain and ticket holders would have to survive the scares on a long, twisting walk along the base of the mountain before ascending by chairlift to the top for the second phase of the haunting.

Ticket holders in groups of eight traveled the haunting together. Five minutes after one group left, another would start. That way every group experienced the thrills without warning. Before each group began, they listened to a computerized skeleton summarizing this year's haunting story line.

The skeleton told of three brothers who become lost in an autumn blizzard on top of the mountain. Bad spirits claimed their bodies and their evil souls took over the mountain. Since then, innocent villagers enjoying hiking or skiing began to disappear. The skeleton urged all visitors to the Ghoulog to exercise extreme caution and to keep their group together at all times, so the evil ones couldn't kidnap an unprotected visitor who lagged behind.

Laughing and screaming, Ellie's group survived the first phase, although their throats became hoarse from reacting to monsters popping up, creatures chasing them and fiends threatening them. Adrenaline flowing, they rode the chair lift to the top of the mountain where a Ghoulog guard told them to follow a dark winding path to an old lodge. All along the path, weird creatures leaped out of the dark, trying to grab them, or lead them off the main trail.

Once inside the old lodge, they found the three brothers doing their evil deeds. In the first room, one grisly brother ran a butcher shop, selling legs, shoulders and back ribs of meat, interspersed with kidneys, liver and brains. Periodically, he would seem to charge in the direction of the observers, startling them into retreat.

In the second room, another brother, dressed as a surgeon, demonstrated for the crowd. On a table before him lay a villager, dressed in a sheet and a ripped-open orange vest. The doctor lifted mounds of intestines and organs from a huge abdominal incision. He explained these succulent goodies would soon be available for sale at his brother's butcher shop. Then a huge alien jumped out of the villager's stomach, scaring Ellie's group into the third room.

There, the third brother displayed how he killed his innocent victims. People were hanging, jerking in death throes. He had bound and gagged others and staked them to the floor; he readied others for dismemberment by chainsaw. Delighting in his work, he piled up the bloody body parts not suitable for sale, preparing to distribute them to the wild porcupines and wolves howling outside the lodge. He warned his guests these ferocious creatures also craved live humans to hunt and eat.

Ghoulog guards then forced Ellie and the others outside, where terrible zombie-like monsters jumped out at them as they made their way back to the chairlift and the ride down to the exit. It was a glorious haunt, horrifying and exciting. Everyone wanted to be a part of it, either as an actor or spectator. Screams filled the air from mountain base to peak every night during October.

EIGHT

FORTUNATELY, THE ONLY real-life scary event this fall was the Greenberg Federal Bank robbery. It was the first major bank robbery in the area and received non-stop coverage by national TV and newspapers. The robbery took place the day after the Brinks' armored truck scheduled delivery of over a million dollars. Usually, the Greenberg Federal Bank held this large amount of money for two days in order to distribute amounts to other banks in the area.

The thieves got away with all of it, over a million dollars. Local newscasts showed the bank's security camera tape repeatedly during September, then a few times in October. The news anchors reminded viewers a generous reward was available for the person who gave information leading to a conviction.

Ellie recorded the gritty black and white film from her television and watched it over and over. She saw six ski-masked robbers in action, securing the tellers, grabbing all incoming customers and forcing them to the floor where the robbers blindfolded them. She shivered when she watched pictures of herself entering the bank and the masked robber pushing her to the floor and blindfolding her. She remembered how cold the floor was and how frightened she had been.

The remainder of the film showed the robbers stuffing money into duffel bags and carrying them out the back door of the bank. Outdoor cameras caught five men jumping into a panel van to escape after the robbery.

Ellie wondered about the sixth man who suddenly disappeared from the film. Why didn't he join the others in the van? Where did he go? She spent hours trying to figure out the mysteries surrounding the bank robbery, working on her computer searching for more information, reading all the reports printed, and questioning anyone who knew the bank workers. She was hoping something she learned would trigger her memory and release the blocked information she held.

A few days after the haunting, James stopped by Ellie's cabin.

He knocked at the door and when Ellie opened it, he could see the flashing of the TV set.

"Hi there. Hope you're not busy. I came by to talk to you about something on my mind. I thought we could take a walk. It's such a beautiful day."

Ellie looked at him, rather dazed. "It is? I didn't notice. I was watching something on the TV."

"Is something wrong? It's not like you to stay inside on a nice day."

"No. Nothing wrong. Just the usual."

"Well, can I come in?"

"Oh, sorry. I didn't mean to be rude. Of course, come on in."

Ellie opened the door wide and stepped back. James had a clear view of the TV as he walked into the living room. A black-and-white movie without sound showed the inside of the Greenberg Federal Bank.

"Ellie. You're not still watching the robbery on the security tape, are you? Do you mind if I turn it off?"

James walked over and turned the TV off. "I'm worried about you."

"I'm fine. I'm just trying to figure this bank robbery out."

"Ellie, it's not just me. Others have noticed, too. Bonnie, Margaret, Sarah and Debbie were at the Pastry Shop this morning. They were all set to drive up here this morning to see what's going on with you."

"What do you mean, 'what's going on with me'? Like what?"

"Now don't get defensive. We're just concerned."

"About what?" Ellie walked into the kitchen, poured two mugs of coffee, added sugar and milk to hers, and handed the black coffee to James.

"Let's sit out on the back screen porch. If it's as beautiful as you say, we can at least talk in the sunlight. I'm afraid this warm weather won't last much longer."

"All the more reason to be out and about now," James said as he made himself comfortable on the porch swing. Ellie sat in a porch rocker and gazed out at the backyard.

"Since the haunting, no one has seen you. You aren't answering your phone. You haven't called Sarah in a week. Frankly, seeing you watching the tape on the TV during a warm fall day really worries me."

"I know. I've overreacted a little, I suppose. Sometimes I come so close to remembering. I think if I try a little harder, I'll have it. Then hours go by and I'm still where I started. It's like a recurring nightmare."

"You have to stop it. By watching the security tape, you're triggering the post-traumatic reaction, in turn stimulating the obsession, and so on. It's a vicious circle, which will just get worse. You have to stop watching the film, stop the research, stop thinking about it, and get busy with your life. Then with no triggers to feed it, the obsession will lessen and eventually fade away."

"But I want to remember."

"You realize working so hard to remember is making your obsession and fear worse?"

Ellie nodded her head. "Yes. You're right. I know you're right. I'm not getting anywhere this way. I'm just making it worse."

Ellie looked at James. "I've felt so shackled to this robbery and the need to solve it; I haven't been able to really become involved in anything or anyone else. If my friends are noticing and you're concerned, then I guess I should pay attention to what you're saying. I better change what I'm doing. They say that insanity's doing the same thing over and over and expecting to get different results."

"That's true," James agreed.

"Your confronting me, telling me straight-out like this, is probably what I need. You've broken my denial, the chain keeping me bound to this mystery."

"I'm sorry you've had to go through so much."

"Me, too. But, to tell you the truth, now that you've intervened, I feel better, relieved. I was living a secret life. I tried to keep away from my friends so they wouldn't worry about me. Now it's out in the open.

"Good. So what are you going to do about it?"

Ellie stood up and walked into the house. When she returned she was holding a DVD.

"This's the bank's security tape. I'm giving it to you. I'm not going to watch it anymore. The TV's staying off just as it used to be. I hardly ever watched TV before. I was too busy having fun in my life."

"Anything else?" James asked as he pocketed the DVD.

"I'm calling my friends and inviting them to dinner and telling them all about what I've been doing. Then I'm going to make plans with them, as I used to. I'm getting back my life, James."

Indeed, Ellie kept her word. She resumed her life with gusto, realizing how much she had missed while she holed up trying to unblock her mind. As October moved into November, Ellie regained her spirit, resumed her outdoor activities, and along with her part-time library work, volunteered to work with some of the children at the Foster's Home for Children.

Eventually, memories of the robbery faded and her fears fled. She felt restored and healthy again.

Local police and the FBI were not able to identify any suspects in the robbery. The thieves disguised themselves too well, spoke little, and left no fingerprints or other forensic evidence behind. The police traced the material of the blindfolds to an out-of-production brand of sheet found in every Goodwill, thrift and used-clothing store across the area. Although the FBI made the case a priority, they made no arrests. As current news took over, the mystery of the robbery faded to snippets on the back pages.

Fall was here in all its glory. The melancholy some folks associated with early darkness, cold nights, and the upcoming change into the icy and snow-laden season was not yet upon the villagers. Instead, growing excitement about seeing the first snowfall of the year was in the air. The townsfolk still had much work to get ready for winter and too much fall fun going on to worry about robberies, blizzards, icy roads, below-zero temperatures and cabin fever.

NINE

Early November:

DEEP IN THE DARK GREEN fir-and-spruce forest, a grove of deciduous trees shivered in the blustery breeze and gave up their last leaves. Yellow-gold, russet, red, orange and dusty brown leaves caught the amber light of the setting sun as they swirled and floated down to the rust-colored pine needles carpeting the forest floor.

They fell on rocks, fallen trees, exposed roots and a form half-hidden behind a rotting log. They spun down on the figure's waxy, white-blue face and on its orange vest, stained with a burgundy crust. They fell into the puncture ripped through the vest and onto raw flesh and exposed innards.

At dusk, the wind increased, driving the leaves along the ground like a mischief of mice as they scuttled up against barriers and could scurry no farther. There they nested into mounds, burying the trunks, lichen-covered rocks, old roots and the body in a colorful shroud.

When the half-moon rose up over the mountains, pale lemon, surrounded by the speckle of millions of stars visible on this cloudless clear evening, the hungry night creatures stirred.

Mice nibbled at the edges of the blood-crusted wound. Slugs, encouraged by the unusually warm

Indian-summer weather, crept over the still body. A fox passed close by, sniffed cautiously, detected the still-strong human scent and moved on. An owl observed from a branch overhead while a murder of crows, black feathers glistening in the moonlight, stood guard from the bare treetops.

Miles away, an old black bear, ravenous with pre-hibernation cravings, sniffed the air and rambled in the direction of the body.

TEN

ELLIE AND BUDDY WERE taking their early-morning walk along the Adams' hiking trail following Foster's Brook as it ambled downhill to join the Coldwater River. Coldwater, white-watered and filled with large boulders and deep swimming holes, veered downhill, eventually forming the huge series of cascades named Hummingbird Falls. Early residents named the falls after the large group of ruby-throated hummingbirds nesting every summer in trees near the edge of the falls.

The water of Hummingbird Falls crashed and roared its way down into the little tourist village of the same name. There, other tributaries joined the mountain stream and together they formed into a fast moving river, which eventually emptied into the Atlantic Ocean. This November morning, thin sheets of ice sparkled at the edges of the water.

Ten years ago, Ellie rented a small cottage in the tiny mountain village of Hummingbird Falls the summer after her husband's death, hoping a change of scene would help her and the children through their loss. During the other three seasons, Ellie taught English at a public high school in the city.

The welcoming acceptance and love the villagers bestowed on the sad little family the first summer encouraged Ellie to rent the cottage the next summer as well. In all, she ended up renting the same seasonal cottage for ten years. Six of those summers her children accompanied her, but Allison and Sandy had been off on their own since graduating from college. Sandy was married with a lovely wife and a one-year-old son in Florida. Allison, still single, was a successful marketing accountant in Chicago.

Last year, Ellie used the generous inheritance Alice Foster, her best Hummingbird Falls friend, bequeathed to her before her unfortunate murder. She hired a local contractor to build a year-round log cabin next to Foster's Brook on the good-sized piece of land Alice left to her. Thanks to Alice's kindness, Ellie retired early and for the first time would experience living year-round in the mountains.

The village locals warned her fall and winter in Hummingbird Falls was unique. Living only ten miles from Mount Franklin, where the mountain observatory reported the most unpredictable weather, lowest temperatures, and highest winds in the country, challenged even the hardiest. Snowfall at the villages tucked at the foot of the mountains averaged over 100 inches a year. Even the most experienced drivers found maneuvering the snow-covered winding mountain roads curving through the icy notches between the peaks dangerous.

But Ellie was as excited as a young girl before her first date at the prospect of spending her first fall and winter in Hummingbird Falls. After all, it was only early November. Indian summer brought warm sunshine and higher than normal temperatures during the day. In spite of all the locals had warned her about, she presumed winter was still far away.

However, she prepared for winter. She bought a

bright red down-filled jacket, new leather-topped boots with fleecy linings, lined leather gloves and a pair of red earmuffs. Ellie stacked flannel sheets and pillow-cases covered with green pine trees and brown moose neatly in her linen closet. A new forest-green down-filled comforter covered her bed. Mike, her farmer friend from up the road, split and delivered four cords of wood, which Ellie was stacking with care near the back screen porch. She bought a new shovel for the steps and walk.

Already, winter chores had started. Every morning Ellie made sure to fill the wood box, the kindling and paper supplies, so they would last until the next day. She filled an old basket with stick matches, fire-starter lighters and a box of book matches. Candles filled another basket. She arranged kerosene lamps on a shelf by the hearth, filled with oil, new wicks and shining glass lamps. She put flashlights of all sizes in each room; extra batteries and flashlights were in the kitchen closet.

Even though Ellie had a propane generator installed which would replace the electricity when wires came down and all power was lost, she also wanted a supply of lamps, flashlights and other backups, just in case the generator failed also. Preparation for emergencies made Ellie comfortable. Her analytical mind could imagine almost any potentially dangerous scenario and the solution to it. She had only to buy the necessities and have them available to feel she had solved those problems in advance.

She stocked her kitchen with canned and dried goods of every kind, including dog food and pounds of chewy treats for Buddy. Gallons of drinking water, crocks full of dry beans, rice, coffee, nuts and dried fruits, and canning jars with every type of vegetable and fruit filled her pantry. Her extra freezer was stuffed full of meat, bread, fish, frozen meals of every description, as well as ice cream, cookies and pies. She would not go hungry no matter what weather hit her this year.

Ellie felt a bit like a bear ready for hibernation. No, more like a homesteader in the Alaskan bush prepared with a six-month supply of goods, which would have to last until the snow melted. Nevertheless, she had only a five-minute drive down into the valley to the village and another twenty-minute drive to a pharmacy, grocery store and super-discount mart. So perhaps her preparations were a bit of overkill. However, she felt ready for whatever came her way.

"What a fine morning, Buddy. Aren't you glad we're out here in all this beauty?" Ellie exclaimed.

Buddy danced alongside her, decorated with a red cotton scarf and a bright neon-orange vest, which matched Ellie's. He stopped and glanced up at her, listening. Seeing her smile crinkle the wrinkles around her full mouth and bright blue eyes and hearing the chipper tone of her voice, Buddy wagged his tail so hard his black-and-white body wriggled with joy.

He barked back to her before resuming his endless sniffing and marking of almost every weed stalk, pinecone, leaf pile or animal scat he came across. It made for a somewhat stop-and-go walk, but Ellie didn't mind because the frequent sniff-and-pee breaks gave her time to catch her breath and look around at spectacular mountain views, old farm meadows and beckoning wooded paths.

They usually walked a half mile down the brook

and then back by the same route each morning. However, two days ago, Ellie stepped on her bathroom scale and determined more exercise and less of the irresistible blueberry turnovers from the Pastry Shop in the village were called for. She didn't consider herself fat, just pleasantly plump, a woman of substance.

Controlling her weight had grown more difficult after she retired. She took more time to bake and enjoyed frequent tea and goodies. Almost every day since she gave up obsessing over her memory block, she visited the Pastry Shop, meeting and gossiping with her friends, drinking hazelnut coffee and eating her favorite blueberry turnovers.

Now her extra pounds made buttoning her corduroy pants and her wool cardigans more difficult. Long walks up and down the steep roads and trails left her puffing and perspiring, her heart racing. She was determined it was time for a change.

No more blueberry turnovers. At least until her pants fit again. In addition, she mapped a new route for their morning walk. She and Buddy would walk a mile down the brook, to the Coldwater River, turn onto an old mile-long cross-country ski path running through the woods, and hike another mile back to her beautiful new log cabin nestled next to Foster's Brook on the edge of the Mountain National Park. This morning was the first time they had taken the new circuit and the second day without a blueberry turnover.

"Here's where we turn, Buddy. Follow the blue blaze marks on the trees and we'll be home in a little while. Then we'll eat our snack. Oh, dear. I mean you'll eat your snack. I'll just drink a cup of raspberry tea, without honey, even."

While Ellie mulled over her commitment to dieting, forming rationalization after rationalization why she should be eating a nutritious, high-antioxidant, energy-boosting, blueberry-filled turnover, Buddy trotted on ahead. He held his nose high in the air, sniffing.

"Buddy, come back here. Stay with me. Don't go so far ahead," Ellie called.

However, Buddy didn't listen to her. His sense of smell was keen and he had detected an irresistible odor. He turned off the path, pushed through the baby balsams lining the edge of the trail and vanished into the thick spruce and fir forest.

"Buddy, Buddy, come here," Ellie yelled. She ran to the spot where Buddy disappeared, puffing with the exertion. The morning air held the scent of balsam needles where Buddy had broken through them. "I don't want to have to come in there after you. Come back. Now."

Buddy was usually a very obedient dog. When he didn't respond to Ellie's call, she knew something unusual had grabbed his attention and he was on the hunt. She called his name repeatedly, but heard only the rustling of dried leaves, the scolding of a little red squirrel perched on a pine branch overhead and the twitter of chickadees as they flitted from tree to tree in search of some seed-laden pinecones.

Then, the "jay-jay-jay" of disturbed blue jays and the warning caw of crows sounded. Looking up she saw three large black crows rising in flight, slowly gaining altitude as they fled. Buddy started barking furiously. Four more crows flew over her, casting shadows as they passed.

ELEVEN

ELLIE WATCHED the crows desert the area and felt a chill shiver up her back. She remembered the phrase, a murder of crows, and the last time she had used the term, in the Greenberg Federal Bank.

That thought cast a dark shadow over the joy she had experienced earlier this morning. She didn't want to think about the bank robbery anymore. She was tired of straining her brain to remember. She wanted to be finished with it. These crows didn't take part in that terrible act. Why did she seem to connect everything to the robbery?

She forced her brain to refocus. She thought about the crows. Ellie had spent quite some time studying crows, fascinated by their behavior. She had watched them soar overhead, light on the tips of trees, then call out forewarning, black-cloaked sentinels. They had an uncanny and powerful ability to anticipate danger. Often after listening to the caucus of crows screaming out, she had found the tracks of a bear or fox, or spied a human hunter who had invaded their territory. The calls these crows made as they flew over her head sounded like warnings.

Something in the woods threatened the crows, bothered the jays, upset Buddy and scared Ellie. She was terrified of leaving the marked trail and becoming lost in the thickly wooded forest. She had heard stories about hikers and hunters who became lost and were never found. Thoughts of murder, the bank robbery, and becoming lost unnerved her. She was uneasy about what she might discover.

However, Ellie wanted to find Buddy. And true to her nature, she was curious about why Buddy ran off and what disturbed the peacefulness of this beautiful morning.

She stepped off the path, brushed through the balsam hedge and followed the sound of Buddy's barking and the jays' jeering. She pushed through pucker brush. Old blackberry canes thick with thorns grabbed at her red wool sweater and orange hunter's vest, keeping her prisoner until she tore herself away. She pushed aside dead branches laced with old spider webs, and jumped when they snapped off with a loud crack. Bushwhacking through the woods was tricky and Ellie couldn't remember a time she had ever walked or hiked off trail. It was hard going and she worked up sweat as she pushed aside the looming branches and moved deeper into the forest. Often, a branch she bent back jolted her as it slammed into her when she let it go too soon.

In her haste, she was careless, tripped on a hidden root and lost her balance. When she recovered her equilibrium, she paused, breathing hard. She could see her breath steaming out of her mouth into the air, which was now rapidly cooling. She hoped the weather wasn't making one of its famous quick changes. Maybe walking this far into the woods wasn't such a good idea. Maybe she should turn back.

Buddy's frantic bark filled the air again. What if he was caught in a hunter's snare or facing off against a porcupine or fisher?

Ellie yelled, "I'm coming, Buddy. Hang on. I'm coming."

She started to run toward the sound of his bark, pushing against limbs of trees blocking her way, snatching at her as she passed. Before she had taken a dozen steps, she felt a painful thud on the back of her head. Her vision blurred and she slipped on the thick carpet of pine needles. Windmilling her arms frantically, but to no avail, she fell to the ground. Her temple struck a leaf-covered rock. Ellie didn't cry out or move. She lay quiet and alone somewhere deep in the forest.

TWELVE

DAVE SHAFFER, Hummingbird Falls's police chief, grabbed the vibrating cell phone as it wriggled across his cluttered desk.

"Yep, it's me. What? Slow down. I can't understand a word you're saying." Dave turned the volume on his cell to high. "Say again." He pushed the phone against his ear, disrupting his carefully combed grey hair.

"You're breaking up, Colby. Where are you?" He shouted, "I can't hear you. Move to higher ground and call again."

Dave slammed the phone on his desk, piled high with papers. He was already irritated and not being able to understand what his deputy said made him even crankier. For the last hour, he had been compiling the bimonthly police report for the town officers, his least favorite task. Delivering the details of the daily work he and officers performed took his time and often his dignity. He groaned and read the draft of his report.

The Hummingbird Falls Police Department attended to the following police-related activities. Responded to a series of gunshots after dark, which turned out to be target shooting. The police chief requested the individual limit target shooting to daylight hours. Received a complaint of criminal mischief. A car window was broken into. Assisted a resident who was locked out of his house. Received a 911 hang-up call. Responded to five false alarms. Arrested an individual with a suspended license. Responded to an accident with a moose. Took a complaint of theft. An arrest was made of an unidentified person who did an impersonation of a government administrator. Assisted a town citizen with the removal of a squirrel from the house. Responded to an accident in the notch. Responded to vandalism of a pumpkin-person. Found and returned two lost dogs. Handled a dispute between some neighbors. Took a lost wallet report. Fingerprinted someone for employment purposes.

He picked the phone up again, flicking the top open. He studied the screen as if it could clear up the problem of Colby's broken-up message for him. He saw nothing but the date, Tuesday, November 8, and the time, 9:46 a.m., and he flipped the phone closed again.

"Damn cell phones. Never work when you need them."

He jumped up and walked to the door. "Rosie, could you come in here?"

"Sure, Chief," a husky voice with just a tinge of Irish answered.

Dave sat back in his well-worn imitation-leather chair and closed his blue eyes for a moment. Despite his gray hair, he looked young for his fifty years. A few wrinkles creased his tanned face and a slight belly strained against his starched white shirt, but he was still a handsome man. He continued to receive flirty looks from some of the women tourists, but after a happy twenty-seven years of marriage with his charming wife, Mary, he remained faithfully enamored with her.

Patrol Officer Rosie O'Rourke peered in the door. "You want me?"

"Come here and give me a hand, will you?" Dave thrust the cell phone at her. "I'm no good on these things. Can you tell where Colby called from?"

"Colby called? When? What's up?"

"I'm trying to find out. The damn phone went dead. I just want to know if he called from his cell or from some other phone. Can you figure it out?"

"Let's see. Shouldn't be too hard. The phone calls you receive are listed under messages. Yeah, Colby called at 9:46 a.m. He used his cell phone. I recognize the number. Call lasted sixteen seconds. He must have been moving into a dead zone."

"Damn dead zones. He was trying to tell me something and then the damn phone just went silent."

"What did he say before the phone conked out?"

"I couldn't really hear him. Something about a truck, a trail, a hurt hunter, some blood, a gun, some kind of trouble was all I could decipher. I just caught a few words. His voice was all broken up."

"Wasn't he headed up the notch this morning?"

"Yeah, up toward the park, along route 46, and on through the notch. He's checking cars illegally parked up there. Out-of-state hunters have been ditching their cars every which way and in clearly designated no-parking areas. He's ticketing them."

"Bringing in our lunch money, good," Rosie laughed.

"Um, yeah." However, Dave wasn't smiling at

Rosie's comment. He was frowning. "I have a feeling something isn't right. His voice sounded, um, I don't know, kind of weird."

Rosie sat up straighter. "What's his speed-dial number?"

"Speed-dial number? Punch four, but I already tried and got nothing."

Rosie punched the tiny keys, her deep green eyes crinkled with concentration. "Let's try again. Maybe he's clear now." She listened and then shook her head.

"Nothing. Roaming, then the message says no service. He must have walked away from the road. Usually there's good cell coverage on the main highway. But get in those woods and up and down some of the ravines and you lose it fast."

"I know. I had Betsy radio his car phone, but he's not responding. I guess you're right. He's left the vehicle for some reason. I think you better drive up there and check it out."

Rosie wrinkled up her forehead as she stared at the wanted posters on the wall. "I wonder why he left his car. Are you worried? There's probably nothing to fret about, but it's strange he left the car and then called you and hasn't called back."

She stood up and tucked her uniform shirt in tightly, then tugged her heavy leather holster belt in place. She walked into the foyer, got her coat, then walked back to Dave's office.

"But, I'm sure he's fine. He's just out of range. He knows how to take care of himself. You think he's okay, don't you?"

Dave asked, "Is there something going on here I should know about? You and Colby, you aren't, um, I mean…"

Rosie interrupted him. "I agree with you, Chief. It's a good idea to take a ride up there and check, just in case, and I should get going. I wouldn't want him needing us and us not responding. The weather's good, warmer than usual right now, so we don't need to worry about that anyway. I can be up there in less than an hour, faster if I use my lights and siren."

"Calm down. I don't want you getting into an accident. I don't think you should speed, but don't dally either. No need for lights and siren."

"Right. I hear you."

"You know weather up there by Franklin can turn in a minute from heaven to hell. So be careful. Call as soon as you spot his car. I don't like it when I can't get in touch with one of you people. Makes me nervous. Especially during hunting season. Anything can happen and usually does."

"I'll be careful, Chief. It's probably just a dead cell phone and we've got all worked up over nothing."

However, Rosie continued to pucker her brow and set her ruby lips in a serious straight line. She pulled on her black fleece-lined leather jacket. She tied her long red hair into a ponytail and covered it with a leather cap with earflaps. The heavy-duty winter gear encased her buff five-foot-ten-inch body. Even so, she was still a good-looking woman. Her freckled nose was perky, her lips a natural bright red, which only further highlighted her smooth, milk-white skin. Large green eyes and thick, dark brown eyelashes completed the look.

"I'll hunt him down. Don't worry," she said with a wave goodbye.

Dave waved back and tried to return to his report, but he couldn't concentrate. He pondered whether Rosie's anxiety indicated Colby and Rosie were lovers. Had their relationship developed into something significant right under his nose? However, nervousness over a fellow officer who was unreachable was justifiable. His own fear came from the inability to contact Colby and not knowing why.

His mind repeated the words he remembered from the brief and broken-up conversation with Colby. *Hunter, trouble, trail, blood, gun* and *truck* were the only words he was sure he heard. No matter how he put those words together, he was apprehensive. He was sure Colby's voice sounded anxious, the tone tight and strained. Although he tried to talk himself out of it, Dave was worried.

He tried to get back to the paperwork on his desk, but was unsuccessful. He looked at his watch, hoping it was time to contact Rosie. He was surprised only five minutes had passed since she had left. It could be hours before she found Colby.

"Damn, why didn't I go myself? I can't stand waiting like this."

He stood up and starting pacing around his office. He kicked the metal wastebasket across the room, spilling its contents everywhere.

"Damn. Face it, man. You're more than worried. You're scared."

THIRTEEN

HUNTING SEASON IN the mountains begins in April with youth turkey hunting, followed by spring wild-gobbler season in May. Black bear and waterfowl season opens in September and lasts three months. In mid-September archers can hunt deer and fall turkeys and small game, including snowshoe, cottontail, squirrel, quail, fox and coyote. In October, turkeys and pheasant are fair game for shotguns. In mid-October, moose are legal with a lottery ticket and deer hunting with muzzle-loaders or firearms begins in early November.

The Hummingbird Falls businesses depended on the money hunters brought in. They knew, as well as the U.S. Fish and Wildlife Service, that the number of hunters had declined sharply in the last ten years. Condominium developments now sprawled on old farmland and new mansions crowded ridge tops. Deer and bear retreated into wildlife preserves where food was available and hunting prohibited, thus discouraging some hunters from traveling into the area. However, business owners in Hummingbird Falls were grateful for the numerous local and out-of-state hunters who still came in late fall, filling motels, restaurants and bars. Those who did travel north to hunt instead of south to Pennsylvania, Virginia or North Carolina, were eager to get away from urban stress and enjoy a weekend roughing it in the woods. They drove into the mountain villages in their big trucks and SUVs, hungry to hunt down wild creatures which otherwise would live peacefully in their serene surroundings.

Jim Sicciana, Andy Green and Bob Nestalli, Taunton, New Jersey, co-workers at the Taunton Brass Works, had been arguing since they finished their breakfast. They were huddled around a fast-dying campfire with the remains of their breakfast scattered about. Burnt toast lay in the ashes, bacon grease solidified on the fire rocks, charred eggshells crackled in the coals, and coffee grounds smoldered on top of the remaining embers. Four empty bottles of Bud rested next to their loaded backpacks.

"Damn it. We've been tromping around these woods for three hours. Haven't even seen so much as a dumb chipmunk. Nothing's here. Let's pack our stuff and go farther up the mountain," Jim growled as he finished off another beer. His large belly strained against the orange hunter's vest under his parka.

Andy, as thin and short as Jim was tall and fat, was scrubbing out the frying pan. Bob, whose stature and appearance was average in every way, was rinsing out the coffee pot, packing up the utensils and leftover breakfast food. They looked at each other. Bob shook his head.

"You know, Jim, if you'd stop yelling and lay off the beer, we might see a bear or a deer. We've seen their crap everywhere and it's fresh. They have to be around here."

Andy broke in. "Yeah, probably right up until they heard us crunching through the leaves on our way up this mountain. The fire and us making so much noise probably chased everything farther uphill."

"We shoulda hooked up with the bear guide we met in the bar last night. His dogs woulda found something by now," Jim said.

"Maybe," Andy answered. "But it didn't seem right to me, sort of like cheating. He sends those dogs out with radio collars and we sit in his heated Jeep, drinking and driving around following the dogs' beeper signal. Then when the beeper stops, we know the dogs treed a bear. All we have to do is get it. That's not what I call hunting."

"What's wrong with it?" Jim asked. "We still have to track the dog through the woods to the treed bear. That's hunting. Then we have to shoot it down."

"Come on, Jim. You've got to be kidding. Three of us shoot a treed bear? How's that hunting? The guide dresses it for us. He takes the claws and the gall bladder to sell as an aphrodisiac on the black market. We split up the head, hide, and any other parts we want and haul them back to the four-wheeler. You call that hunting?"

"Jesus, that's the way it's done today," Jim answered.

"It's not how I do it," Bob said. "If I'm hunting, then I'm hunting the way my dad did, not riding around waiting for a red tick hound's beeper to tell me what to do."

"Oh, so the shiny brand-new semi-automatic with a scope you're carrying was your dad's?"

"You know what I mean, Jim. Stop being such a wiseass. You know he used an old muzzle-loader."

"Okay," Andy intervened. "What're we going to do now? I'm already tired of carrying this heavy pack. I brought too much stuff. Let's leave our packs here and travel light. We can come back and cook our lunch later, just before dusk. We can move faster and hunt farther out, but get back to the truck before it gets too dark."

"You know the plan, Andy. We said we'd hunt from dawn to nine, rest and eat, then pack up and move to a new location if we didn't see any bear or deer. Well, we haven't seen any. And we'd just spend time backtracking old territory if we leave our packs here and have to come back. Let's take our packs, head out and bushwhack back to the truck later. What are you? A wimp? Can't carry a pack?"

"Stop it, Jim," Bob said. "No reason to start bad-mouthing. We partied too much last night, got a late start, and if you feel like I do, you've got a whooping headache."

"Not me, man. Hair of the dog fixed my pains. I'm feeling ready to go. Have another beer. It'll take your headache away. Plus, it's less to carry."

"There's only a few left. Let's leave them for when we come back," Andy said.

"I'm taking my share with me," said Jim. "I get thirsty. And I'm taking my pack, too. You guys can leave yours here for all I care. I'm not hunting used ground. It's a waste of time. If we don't find anything in the next hour or so, maybe I'll make my own way and meet you back at the truck later."

"If a game warden finds you with beer, your ass'll be fried."

"Stop being such a jerk. We came up here to have fun. If I can't shoot a deer or a bear, then I might as well get a buzz on."

"All right, if you want to take your pack, go ahead. I'm leaving mine here," said Andy.

Bob looked from one man to the other. "I guess I'm with Andy. I'd rather come back here. At least I know the way back to the truck from this spot. I'm not too good at bushwhacking and I don't really like the idea of splitting up. We might end up shooting each other."

Jim checked out the backpacks, moving some stuff around, while Bob climbed up a maple tree. Andy threw up a cord so they could rope their heavy packs over a tree branch ten feet from the ground.

"That'll keep the animals out of them," Andy said.

"What about the squirrels, stupid?" Jim sneered.

"They're hibernating, aren't they?" Andy asked.

Jim laughed. "My God. You really are a city boy, aren't you?"

"Come on, you two," Bob said. "And shut up, will ya? I don't know about you, but I'd like to bring something home to show my kids and prove to the wife I really was hunting. Then maybe she'll let me come next year."

They laughed and with spirits somewhat restored, they picked up their Remington semi-automatics and stumbled down the trail. Dressed in orange and red from head to toe, they carried their rifles and wore large leather waist belts holding extra ammunition, knives and nine-millimeter Glock sidearms. They had stuffed their day packs with cell phones, handyman all-in-one tools, water bottles, compasses, flashlights and snacks for energy. Jim carried his fully loaded backpack as well. They were a walking advertisement for L.L.Bean. Totally outfitted, a combination of hunter-camper-hiker-outdoorsman, complete with every piece of gear available, the three men were off on their fall hunt.

FOURTEEN

THE OLD BEAR STRUGGLED down the slippery granite slabs. His left front paw, injured years before by a steel foot trap, seized up with arthritis in the damp cold. Once graceful and coordinated, the bear's range of motion was now limited and he fell often as he clambered to the bottom of the slope. When he reached level ground, he lay down and whimpered. His long agile tongue licked at the old wound in an attempt to relieve the pain.

At five hundred pounds, the bear was over average size for an adult wild male black bear and measured seven feet long from nose to tail. He was eighteen years old and had lived longer than the majority of wild black bears. Wild bears usually die before they reach eleven, victims of human-related causes. Most often, hunters killed them. Some were hit by cars or poisoned. However, starvation, accidents and infected wounds from fighting other bears caused death, too.

This old bear could no longer see long distances, but his hearing and ability to smell remained intact, exceeding human ranges. His intelligence was still keen; his large brain and excellent long-term memory functioned well. Due to his age, heavy winter weight and reduced mobility, he no longer could run thirty miles per hour, but he could still swim over a mile in the cold lakes.

His shaggy winter hair was slightly silvered, mangy and crusted in places. A long scar from a tangle with another bear replaced the fur on the side of his face, giving him an odd twisted look. Those who had sighted him over the years nicknamed him Old Scar Face.

This fall had been hard on him. His preferred foods—nuts, acorns, fruit, insects and greens—were scarce due to limited rainfall, and he failed to add the optimal amounts of fat necessary to hold him through the long months of hibernation, soon to come. Because of his age and injuries, Old Scar Face arrived late at his usual feeding spots and didn't fill his hungry stomach. The old blueberry fields he once commanded were picked clean by the time he arrived. Competitors had already consumed the cherries, blackberries, acorns and apples he depended upon to push his fat content to its fullest extent and ready him for hibernation. Other bears and deer, squirrels, chipmunks, birds, fox, mice and all types of insects had benefited from the food, which would have kept Old Scar Face from starving.

His instinct for survival controlled him now, forcing him to forage far from his home territory into unfamiliar grounds. Like most male black bears, Old Scar Face traveled alone. Food was too limited for him to hunt with other adult black bears. In this territory new to him, he now faced possible competition with unknown males and his scarred face, head, shoulders and forelegs clearly proved he had survived many fights in his lifetime.

Old Scar Face's big teeth, long claws, enormous strength and large size made him seem the perfect predator. However, he rarely caught anything alive larger than insects. The few live prey he did manage to catch and devour were mainly nestling birds, newborn mammals, penned livestock, or spawning fish. This fall, Scar Face had caught few of those.

Like all black bears, he prized carrion or dead flesh of any sort and its attractiveness increased with its degree of decomposition. His long canine teeth easily tore apart the rotting flesh. His lips, unlike those of other animals, were free from his gums and he used them with amazing dexterity, whether licking out the marrow of bones, eating tiny blueberries or slurping up ants out of rotting logs.

As fierce as Old Scar Face looked, his fearsome reputation was largely unfounded. He was ordinarily timid around humans, with a non-confrontational disposition, and usually ran away if he heard or smelled humans nearby. If startled or cornered, he would stand his ground and bluff, especially when extreme hunger drove him, but he intentionally bit or clawed only in self-defense or when fighting another bear for a mate or territorial rights.

Old Scar Face finished tending to his paw and got up, sniffing. Detecting an interesting odor, he stood on his hind feet, trying to locate the direction of the tantalizing smell. Down again on all fours, the huge bear loped in the direction of the carrion scent.

FIFTEEN

ELLIE FELT A WET COOLNESS soothing her aching head. She lay still, unwilling to interrupt the comforting action. However, when the cold wet moved from her forehead to her lips, then to her ears and neck, she forced her eyes open.

Leaning over her was Buddy. He was licking her face.

"Oh, Buddy. What happened?" she whispered as she tried to sit up. She lay back down.

"Ouch, my head hurts."

She raised her arm and pulled off her wool cap. She felt her head where it was pulsing most painfully. She found a large bump. She looked at her hand.

"At least it's not bleeding," she mumbled. "Something or someone must have really walloped me."

Then she noticed her forehead hurt, too. When she touched the injured place on her temple, she gasped with pain. Blood smeared her fingers.

"Oh, dear, I guess I hit my head going down, too. I'm bleeding."

Ellie raised herself slowly onto her elbows, gasping as the pain and pounding in her head increased. Blood slowly dripped down the side of her face.

"Wow. My head really hurts, Buddy. Come close. Let me hold on to you so I can sit up." She grabbed Buddy's fur and pulled herself to a sitting position. She leaned against his back and held on until the dizziness passed.

When she lifted her head, she noticed the woods had grown darker. Clouds covered the sun. The air had chilled down since earlier this morning. Buddy's moist breath had formed small icicles around his nose, whiskers and mouth.

Ellie shivered. "I wonder how long I've been unconscious. It isn't dusk already, is it?" She moved carefully and glanced around. "I hope the blow on my head didn't affect my eyes, Buddy. Everything looks dark."

Then she saw the rock she had hit. Smudges of blood were frozen in red ice on the leaves covering most of its surface.

"Lucky for me, leaves softened the rock a little. Otherwise, I might be worse off than I am. Well, I can see the rock and leaves well enough, so I guess my eyes must be okay. But it's getting so dark. Either I was out for hours or the weather's changing."

Ellie looked up again. Through spaces between the treetops, she could see huge clouds blacking out the blue sky she and Buddy enjoyed earlier today. Gusts of cold wind were whipping branches back and forth. Black crows rode the bucking limbs, fighting for balance. Occasionally one would raise a flapping wing to keep the wind from tossing him off while another clamped his feet tightly like stirrups into the bark of the heaving branch.

"The crows are back, Buddy. Good or bad omen? What do you think? Probably bad because it looks like nasty weather's on its way. You're going to have to help me, dear Buddy. I think we need to get home."

Buddy whined. He bit down on her vest and tried to pull her along the ground.

"Wait a minute. Hold on there, Buddy. Don't worry. We'll beat the storm. I'll get up soon. Just let me get oriented a little."

She patted Buddy's fur. He sat down next to her and whined. He hated storms and wind. The vibrations bothered his ears and Ellie usually covered his head with a pillow or blanket until the storm was over. Now he was panting and nervous.

Between gusts of wind, she noticed the smell. The odor was so putrid Ellie put a hand over her nose and pinched her nostrils closed.

"Peeyou! Something must have died. What a dreadful smell. That's what made you run in here, isn't it, boy? Well, we've got to get away from that disgusting odor. It's making me sick to my stomach and my head ache even more."

Ellie pulled the red cotton scarf from her neck and wiped the drying blood off her face. She was relieved to find the bleeding had slowed. Then she tied the scarf over her nose, hoping to reduce the awful smell making her nauseous. She glanced at Buddy's matching scarf, tied around his neck, above his orange dog vest.

"What's smeared on your vest? Oh, no. It looks like blood! Are you hurt, Buddy? Did something hurt you, too?"

Ellie rubbed her hand over Buddy, but found no wounds or injuries. "You aren't hurt, boy, but you sure smell bad. Where did you get so stinky? Oh, dear, I've got a bad feeling, Buddy, you got it from whatever attracted you in here. Did you roll on something dead?"

Buddy whined and stood up, turning around and facing in the direction of the putrid odor.

"Show me," Ellie demanded. Using Buddy as a

support, she slowly pulled herself to her knees. Vertigo swept her again. She closed her eyes and kept her hand pressed on Buddy's back until the whirling passed. Then she stood up slowly and looked around, her head spinning with dizziness again. When she opened her eyes this time, she saw a mound of leaves on the far edge of the small clearing. Buddy seemed to be pointing in that direction.

Slowly, she made her way over to the leaf pile. Holding her breath to avoid breathing in the horrid odor, she lowered herself to her knees and brushed some of the leaves aside. She was staring at a face. A face she had seen before.

Blank, glazed opaque eyes stared back at her. Lower down the body, she spied the blood-dried open wound and exposed innards, rotted and mangled. She flung herself away, gasping for air. She clasped her hands over her scarf-covered mouth and nose.

"Oh, no. Oh, how awful. Oh, oh. I think he's dead. What should we do? We've got to find someone, tell someone. This's terrible. He's got to be dead."

Ellie managed to sit up and push herself back from the body, her head churning with pain and confusion from trying to take in everything: the bump on her head, the cut on her temple, the growing darkness and cold, the approaching storm. and the dead body hidden under the leaves.

She was in the middle of the woods, injured, a storm on the way, alone except for Buddy, a dead body and maybe a murderer or a rogue bear. For certainly, someone or something killed this man.

She mused about the body. If it had been here a long time, it had probably frozen and thawed dozens of times with the up-and-down temperature of the fall weather. Yesterday and today's Indian-summer warmth would encourage further breakdown of tissue and flesh, producing the horrible smell making Ellie ill. Or, maybe someone recently dumped the body here and it hadn't had time yet to lose its flesh and smell.

Panic gripped her. She remembered she left the trail to find Buddy. But how far into the woods had she come? Could she find her way back? Could she walk far enough to reach home? The terrible pain in her head, the awful dizziness and inertia, demanded that she lie down and sleep.

She glanced again at the man, willing herself to unblock and recall who he was. But all she saw was a man who was very, very dead.

She looked around, searching. Somewhere his killer lurked. Ellie trembled. Was he watching her? Was he here?

SIXTEEN

ROSIE DROVE the black Hummingbird Falls police SUV north on Route 46 toward the notch between Madison Mountain and Jefferson Ledge. Traffic was light this morning. The leaf-peepers had left to travel farther south for the prime color spots. Most hunters entered the woods to stalk their prey by first light of dawn. They parked their vehicles all along the highway and pulled into lots that hikers used in summer. She looked in each lot for Colby's vehicle, which matched the one she was driving.

As she came around the turn where the Elton River surged close to the road, she spied a group of cars parked illegally in a field abutting the river. She could see tickets flapping on windshields of Massachusetts, New York, New Jersey and Michigan vehicles. New Hampshire vehicles filled the legal parking spots in the designated lot. Colby had been here.

She kept on driving. At the next trailhead parking lot, most drivers parked in designated spaces, but several vehicles parked on the side of the highway, which was not legal. Tickets decorated the windshields of those lawbreakers.

As Rosie continued driving farther north, she noticed the sun disappear behind some ominous-looking clouds filling the sky. Her radiophone crackled with static.

"Rosie. Where are you? Any sign of Colby?"

"Signs of him everywhere, Chief. He's been working hard. Must have tagged about thirty vehicles by now. Mostly New Jersey and New York, as usual."

"Have you spotted his vehicle?"

"That's a negative, Chief. I'm following the ticket trail. Next lot up is Dalia's Place Trail. Maybe he's there."

"Call me as soon as you spot his car."

"Will do. Weather looks like it's turning bad. Have you got the forecast?"

"Yep. The observatory on top of Franklin just reported fifty-mile-per-hour winds, driving snow and temp's about twenty degrees and falling. They expect the squall to roll down slope and hit the valley shortly. What's it like where you are?"

"Starting to look like we're going to get some of the white stuff. Sun's buried under a huge black cloud. Did they say how much or how long?"

"Nope. Just called it a squall, closed down the auto road to the peak and put out an advisory to all hunters, hikers, campers and climbers. You know the observatory can't predict the weather, they can only tell us what's happening now. Too variable up there."

"Yep. Well, I hope everyone up here came equipped. Otherwise, there's going to be frozen toes and fingers. Okay, I'm at Dalia's. Tickets, but no Colby. Looks like he tagged ten cars here. Next stop, Wilson's Folly. I'll call you when I catch up with him."

Rosie continued driving through the steep notch. She flipped her headlights on as the morning turned dark. The wind picked up and she held the steering wheel firmly to keep from swaying with the wind gusts. Spits of snow hit her windshield and whirled away. As she rounded a sharp curve, she could see a few cars up ahead at the Wilson's Folly parking lot. She slowed down.

The Hummingbird Falls police SUV was parked in the lot, blocking a large V8, four-wheel-drive truck with a New Jersey license plate. The only other vehicles parked were two trucks with New Hampshire plates. They were parked legally, and not ticketed.

Rosie drove into the lot and parked beside Colby's car. She peered into the car, but didn't see Colby. She turned off her engine and looked around. No sign of him. She sighed. She'd have to get out in the windy cold and track him down.

Before she did anything, Rosie reported to Dave. "I've found his car in the Wilson's Folly lot, but he's not in it. I'm getting out to look around. See if I can spot him."

"Any other vehicles in the lot?"

"Positive on that. Colby's vehicle's blocking a black Dodge Ram four-wheel-drive cab, license tag NJ 354986. Looks like he didn't want them to leave. Two other trucks are in the lot. A green Chevy pickup, NH CA9756, and a red Ford pickup, NH CA2646. No tickets on either of them."

"Be careful. I don't want both of you missing. If you see anything which looks suspicious, get back to your vehicle and call me. Got it?"

"Yes, sir. I'll call you and I'll be careful, but nothing looks out of order so far."

"Let's hope it stays that way. I'll be waiting for your call. Good luck."

"Yes, sir." Rosie pulled on her gloves and hopped out of the SUV, locking the door after her. The freezing wind spat snowflakes, small and hard as sand, into her face. She pulled up her coat collar, pulled down her earflaps and fastened the chinstrap of her hat. As she looked around, three men dressed in hunters' orange walked out of the woods and headed to the New Hampshire trucks. She intercepted them.

"Morning. I'm Officer O'Rourke. How ya doing?"

"Okay," one of the hunters replied. "Didn't find any deer, though. Looked like a storm's on the way, so we decided to try somewhere closer to town."

"Good idea. By the way, did you see another officer on the trail?"

"Nope. We took the trail up a ways when we first came in, say about three hours ago, around 8:00 a.m., but when we started back down, we pushed through the woods, hoping we'd get a deer on the way. Didn't see a soul or a deer. Your officer get lost?"

"No. Just trying to catch up with him. I need to see your hunting licenses and truck registrations, then you can go."

The men complied and Rosie took their information down. "You take it easy now. This storm's moving fast. It could really dump a lot of snow on us. By the way, did you see the occupants of that black Ram when you came in this morning?"

Rosie pointed to the black truck.

"Nope. We were the first ones here. Should've taken it as a sign this wasn't the best place to hunt, I guess. Next time we'll park where everyone else is."

Rosie forced a tight smile. "Okay. Thanks. Drive safely."

The men nodded, loaded their gear into the two trucks and pulled out of the lot.

The only vehicles left were two Hummingbird Falls police SUVs and the truck Colby had blocked.

Rosie looked in Colby's windows, but nothing indicated where he was or that anything was wrong. Then she examined the big black truck Colby had blocked.

Did Colby park to stop the truck from leaving? Did he see something, which made him leave his vehicle in a hurry, not noticing he was blocking the truck? Did he spot something about the truck or its occupants that made him wary?

She looked at the license tag. It was newly issued from New Jersey, up-to-date and spotlessly clean, like the outside of the truck. Why didn't Colby call in the tag earlier?

All she had were questions. She tried to open the driver's door, but it was locked. Rosie pulled herself up on the step on the driver's side and peered in the front window. The tinted glass made it hard to see in, but she noticed maps, scattered newspaper pages, empty take-out coffee cups, fast-food and candy-bar wrappers littering the floor. She thought she spied a liquor bottle stashed under the passenger's seat, but she couldn't see clearly enough from where she was. She glanced through the dark glass into the backseat.

She gasped. If Colby looked into the truck's backseat, he would have been as horrified as she was. He would have made sure the black truck couldn't leave. That is, if he looked inside, and not been pushed inside by someone, who...

She couldn't finish the thought. She jumped down off the step, ran around to the other side of the truck and tried the doors. Locked. She looked in the back window. No question what was in the backseat. And it scared her to death.

SEVENTEEN

ROSIE RAN BACK to her vehicle and called Dave.

"Chief. There's trouble. Bad. Real bad."

"Take it easy, Rosie. What's happening?"

"The Ram truck. The backseat. Blood all over it."

"Is it Colby? Is he hurt? Should I send an ambulance?"

"No. No. He's not in the truck. I haven't seen him."

"Thank God. I thought you were going to tell me he was hurt. Why didn't you say that first?"

"I don't know. But this doesn't look good. There's a mess in the backseat. Lots of blood, seat's ripped up, some bloody clothes."

"Is there a body?"

"No. Not in sight, anyway. The clothes in the backseat don't look like Colby's, at least I don't think so. He had his uniform on, didn't he?"

By this time, Rosie was hyperventilating and her voice was rising into what soon might be a quavering wail.

"Yep, full uniform. Okay, let's take a breath. Take another. Calm down. Let's take it one step at a time, Rosie. Are you with me?"

"Yes," Rosie answered, her voice trembling, but in normal range.

Dave continued. "Colby's SUV's there, but he's not.

The bloody clothes in the backseat of the truck don't appear to be his. But that's all we know, right now. Right?"

Dave could hear Rosie take another deep breath.

"I hear you." Another intake of air and then Rosie said, "Inspection sticker's recent and looks legit. But Colby's not here. He must have checked the truck for violations and either saw the backseat and took off up the trail, or maybe he saw someone beating on someone and got involved somehow. Either way, it looks bad. Colby would've called us. You know that, Chief. He would've called if he could."

"Take it easy, Rosie. He did call, but not from the parking lot or the reception would've been okay. He called from a dead zone. So we can assume he was okay up to when his cell stopped working. That has to be some distance from where you are. Describe what you saw in the truck again."

"Front seat trashed up with take-out wrappers, newspapers, I think from the city, maybe the Globe. Otherwise, nothing, but maybe a liquor bottle under the seat. The backseat. Well, it's covered with blood, looks recent, not all dried. The seats are ripped open in places, like with a knife, I think. Clothes thrown around, a shirt, towel and a T-shirt, all bloody. It looks like a massacre. Someone lost a lot of blood. What do you want me to do?"

"Keep breathing. Betsy's running the tags as we speak. I'm on my way up there now. I'm going to pull Larry and a couple of the guys off the road crew and bring them with me, just in case."

"What do you want me to do, Chief?"

"Check the rest of the lot, the porta-johns and the trailhead. See who's signed in and out and be careful."

"Okay, will do. Oh, I forgot. I didn't spot any ticket

on the truck. And, I talked to three hunters coming out of the woods just before I looked inside the truck. They didn't see anyone, or hear anything suspicious. I took their names and license numbers, just in case. But they seemed clean, legit. No other cars here."

"Good work. Now go look at the places I mentioned. Then call me back."

"Chief, if I don't find Colby down here, I'm going to hike up the trail a bit and see if I can locate him. I'll try my cell up higher. It might work if he's close enough. I brought the two-way. He probably has his buckled on. If I don't reach him by cell, I'll try the two-way. I'll get back to you as soon as I can."

"Hey, Rosie, listen to me. Before you go to the trail-head, put some crime tape around the truck, so no one bothers it. And be careful what you touch."

"I had my gloves on. I only touched the door handles and the windows when I looked in. But I'll fasten the tape and put the police-area sign up before I go. Anything else?"

"Be careful out there, Rosie. If Colby met up with something he didn't expect, he might be in trouble."

Rosie interrupted. "Dave, what if…"

Dave broke in. "No what-ifs. Don't go there, Rosie. It'll only mess you up. You've got to keep alert. Colby's experienced and knows what to do if there's trouble. I only said he might be in trouble as one possibility. Most likely, he's okay, just not able to contact us."

"Yes, sir."

"I don't want you in danger, too. If you don't think you can handle this alone, then stay in your car until I get there."

"I'm okay, Chief. Just for a moment there, I kinda, well, got ahead of myself. I'm ready to go now."

"I know you, Rosie. You're capable of taking the lead on this until I get there. If you see something—anything—that bothers you, back off and call me. If anything looks weird, makes you wary, get back to the SUV and wait for me. I don't like you out alone with all those hunters and whoever else may be running around. Hunters tend to shoot at anything that moves. And negative on going up the trail. Don't go up the trail. No farther than the trailhead. Got it? When I get there, we'll go together."

"Sorry, Chief. But I'm slipping an orange vest over my coat as we speak, just in case. The hunters will spot me for sure. Plus, I'll be yelling Colby's name so loud, everyone'll know I'm coming. Chief, I'm sorry. I can't wait for you. It'll take you at least an hour to get here. That might be too long. Colby could be, well, he may need some help before you can get here. I'm going to hike on up the trail, if I don't find him down here."

The radiophone was silent for a moment. Then Dave's voice spoke softly.

"Okay, Rosie. Do what you have to. I'd do the same if it were me. But be careful. Watch your back. I'll be there as soon as I can. Keep in touch."

Rosie wrapped an extra scarf around her neck and pulled her leather gloves on over a pair of wool ones. She put the first-aid emergency kit into her backpack along with a flashlight, hand warmers, energy bars, an aluminum blanket and extra water. Her sidearm, knife, baton and two-way were strapped around her waist. She slipped ice cleats onto her boots, took her hiking sticks, donned the backpack and set out to wrap the New Jersey truck in crime-scene tape. She secured the tape well against the gusting wind and fastened the DO

NOT TOUCH: POLICE EVIDENCE sign on the bumper. Then she jogged toward the trailhead. She couldn't wait for Dave and the crew. She had to do all she could to find Colby.

Rosie searched the porta-john area. No sign of Colby. She walked to the trailhead and took the sign-up book from inside the wooden box labeled with the directive: Everyone Using This Trail Must Sign in and Out. Just as she started to scan the names, she noticed splotches wetting the paper.

She looked up. Snow. The spitting of occasional small flakes had spun into a shower of larger flakes driven horizontally by the wind. The front arrived in full force. The temperature started dropping. The wind-chill factor must be in the danger zone.

Rosie pulled her collar higher to keep the snow from sneaking down her neck. She turned back to the list. Everyone had signed out with exit times, except one. At the bottom of the list, she saw Colby's name. The time he signed in was 9:33 a.m. He hadn't signed out. Rosie guessed he had called Dave from somewhere on the trail, then, thirteen minutes after he signed in. She'd have to walk approximately thirteen minutes to arrive at the place they last heard from him. She signed her name and the time, 11:08 a.m., and started up the trail.

The snow intensified as she trudged along the steep winding path. Already white snow covered the brown of dead leaves and dirt trail. She checked her watch. Another minute to go. She saw and heard nothing but the splatter of heavy snow on dry leaves, the chitter of birds and the chatter of squirrels and chipmunks.

The snow was accumulating fast. She looked back down the trail. Her footsteps were filling in, disappearing, as she watched.

At 11:21 a.m., she stopped and looked around. She yelled, "Colby," but her words just whipped away with the wind.

She pulled her red wool scarf up to keep the bitter gusts from blasting her face. Visibility was decreasing now. She couldn't see very far ahead of her up the trail and couldn't see at all off trail where wet, white snow was quickly coating the trees.

She turned in a circle, searching. Nothing. She scraped some snow off the path with her boots, a foot this way, a couple of feet that way. She wasn't sure what she was looking for, but she must be close to the spot from where Colby called. She took a few steps farther up the trail and scuffed at the snow again. She walked, kicking snow away from the path toward the woods.

She tried the cell phone. The screen told her once more, no service. She continued walking slowly up the trail. Then she saw something.

A small snow-covered mound sat right in the center of the trail. It could be a rock or a branch, disguised by the snow cover, but she moved toward it as fast as she could. She kicked at the snow. Something red stopped her. She bent down. Slowly with her gloved hands, she scooped the snow away.

A red wool cap with the initials HFPD in black lay half-buried. Colby's cap. She picked it up and shook the snow off. She studied the hat, turning it in her hand, examining every inch. Along the edge of the fold, she found a dark stain. Rosie pulled her gloves off. She rubbed her finger over the stain. Her finger turned red. Blood red.

EIGHTEEN

"Damn, it's cold. And now it's snowing. Just yesterday, it was almost fifty degrees. This state's crazy. How could anyone live where the temperature drops thirty degrees in just a few hours? Let's get outa here and head for a place where we can get hot burgers, fries and beer. I'm through," Jim groused.

He struggled out of his backpack and threw it on the ground.

Bob and Andy looked at each other, shaking their heads. "The snow'll help. Their tracks will lead us right to them," said Bob. "And it'll keep us from making so much noise on these crunchy leaves."

"But we have to find the tracks first," Andy added. "So pick up your pack and let's get going."

"Have you got any of those heat pads? My hands are frozen," Jim said as he slapped his hands together. "I think these gloves are too small. My blood isn't getting to the ends of my fingers."

"They're back in my pack," Andy said.

Jim cursed. "Of all the things to leave behind, first the beer and then the heating pads. What's wrong with you?"

"I didn't think we'd need them. The sun was out and I thought we'd be sweating climbing those ravines."

"Well, you thought wrong. I'm freezing, not sweating. Why did I ever come on this hunt in the first place?

Nothing but suffering," Jim plopped down on a rock. "I'm outa beer, too. Figures."

He bent over, holding his hands under his armpits and stamping his feet in the accumulating snow. "Who knew it would snow and get so cold?"

"Not me," Bob said. "The weather report I heard this morning said sunny and in the forties or fifties. It sure ain't sunny and with the wind-chill factor it's got to be way below freezing."

"Duh," said Jim. "It's snowing. It's got to be below freezing."

"I tried to call the weather station on my cell a few minutes ago, but I just get a roaming and out-of-service message," said Andy.

"Where are we, anyway? Where's the map? I want to see how long it'll take us to get back to the truck," Jim asked.

"I'll try my cell," said Bob. He pulled the cell out of his day pack. "Uh-oh. Battery's dead. I guess it's too cold. Sucks the batteries."

Jim tried his cell phone. "I've got some battery, but no service. Where are we anyway? In some third-world country? Don't they have cell service up here?"

Bob pawed through his day pack. "I haven't got the map. Andy, I gave it to you the last time we checked it, back at the place we had breakfast."

"No, you didn't. I handed it back to you."

"No. I saw you put it in your day pack. Trust me. It's in there."

Andy searched through his pack. He searched all his pockets. "I don't have it. I know I gave it back to you, Bob. Look again."

Bob started to search all his pockets, inside his jacket and out. "Jim, did I give the map to you?"

"I don't know. I don't think so."

"Well, look, damn it. We've got to have the map to find our way back."

Jim heaved himself up off the rock. "Shit, my pants are all wet. I hate snow." He kicked at the rock. "Ow, my toes are numb. I'm freezing to death. Let's get a fire going."

"Look for the map," Bob demanded. "I don't have it. You must have taken it from Andy."

Jim unzipped his pack and started pulling things out and throwing them onto the ground in the snow. He mumbled as he did it, identifying each object. "Socks, sweater, trail mix, camera, flashlight, extra gloves, book…"

"Book? You carried a book all the way up here?" Andy gasped.

"Yeah. I did. Although it's none of your business what I carry or don't."

"What the hell is the title of a book so precious you'd haul its extra weight on a hunting trip?" Bob asked.

"None of your business either," Jim growled.

Bob took a swipe at the book and Jim jerked it away. Andy jumped on Jim, grabbed the book and they both fell to the ground. Andy lay on his back laughing as he read the title aloud.

"*Survivor Tools*. God, it's a hardbound library book. It's got to weigh five pounds. Why'd you bring this?"

Jim pushed him off and stood up. He held his gloved fists out in front of him.

"Come on. Get up. I don't want to knock you out while you're down."

"Stop it, stop. Andy, get up and give Jim back his

book. Sorry, Jim. It's really none of our business what you've got in your pack."

"You're damn right." Jim glowered at Andy.

"Sorry, Jim. I was just trying to have some fun."

"Well, have it with someone else. This's no fun. And if you want to know, my wife made me bring this. She got it at the library. The only way she'd let me come up here in the wilderness was if I took this book with me. She was afraid I'd get stuck up here. The way things look, maybe we will."

Jim threw the book into his pile of belongings. The wind picked up. The snow thickened and the day grew darker and colder. The three men stood, their backs to the wind, looking at the swirling white snow sweeping past them, covering everything in its path.

"We better start back," Andy said. "The snow's getting worse. Who knows how long it'll keep up?"

Jim bent over and shoved the items he had emptied out of his pack back into it, not bothering to brush off the snow. He zipped it up, heaved it onto his back, and fastened the straps.

"I'm ready. Which way?"

They all looked around. Everything had changed in just a few short moments. The leaf-covered brown ground was now solid white. The fir trees were bending under their loads of white snow, closing them in. Midday looked like dusk. They could only see a few yards ahead of them.

"I'll get my compass," Bob volunteered. "You know how to work it, right Andy?"

"Me? No, not really. The guy at the store said there were directions in the package, but I threw it away. I thought you knew how to read a compass."

"I know if the arrow points to N, that's north. But

what good does that do without a map? I don't know where the nearest road is, north or south."

"No, I don't believe it. Don't tell me you guys don't know where we're at," Jim yelled.

"Shut up. Yelling doesn't help," Andy said. "We just have to backtrack. We came from there, right?" He pointed downhill.

"I guess so," Bob agreed. "We were walking uphill, right?"

"Yeah, guys. We've been walking uphill and downhill and uphill and downhill all morning. But, which direction?"

"It makes sense to just go downhill. We'll hunt for the trail as we go down. We'll hit it in a few miles. No problem. But let's get going before the snow gets any deeper."

Bob started off, moving with his back to the wind, downhill. As he brushed by snow-covered limbs, the branches unloaded their mantle of snow on him. Cursing, he pulled up his collar and pulled down his cap. The snow down his neck melted against his sweating skin, causing a chill to run up his back. He hunted for some sign they had passed this way.

The others followed him single file, trying to step in his tracks to avoid getting snow in their shoes. Several inches of heavy snow lay on the ground now. As Andy looked back over his shoulder, he could see their footsteps filling in. Soon, all traces of them would disappear. He hoped Bob was leading them in the right direction. He knew he didn't have a clue where they were, or how far they had come, one mile or ten. He was lost. In fact, he worried they might all be lost.

NINETEEN

OLD SCAR FACE SHAMBLED into the hunter's breakfast campfire site just as the snow started to fall. He ignored the human scent and went straight for the bacon grease. His long tongue lapped the lard from the rocks. He clawed the toast bits and eggshells from the ashes and consumed them, but left the coffee grounds alone. He snuffed up crumbs from the ground as fast as he could before the snow buried them forever. When he finished cleaning up the breakfast garbage, he looked around for more. His appetite was stimulated, not appeased, by the humans' food.

He sniffed the cold air and a faint scent led him to the skeletal branches of the maple. He stood on his haunches and swiped at the backpacks hanging there. He managed to get one down with no problem. With his long claws, he sliced the canvas open and snuffled inside for the apples, chips, sandwiches, cookies and cheese. He gobbled down the food, plastic wrappings and all. When it was gone, he tossed around the clothes and other objects, trying to find more. A paper map, stained with bacon fat, occupied him for a few minutes as he chewed up the grease-soaked paper.

Old Scar Face dug his sharp claws into the maple-tree bark and hoisted himself up the trunk to the other backpack. He tussled with it until he had severed the strap and the backpack fell to the ground. He jumped down and ripped it open. Easy pickings for the old bear.

When he had consumed everything edible, Old Scar Face bit into the green pack and whipped it back and forth as if trying to break its neck and kill it. When he was satisfied he had defeated the green enemy, he repeated the frenzy with the orange backpack. He didn't stop until both were shredded.

He nosed around the fire site some more. He shook the snow off his heavy coat and sniffed into blowing wind. It was difficult for him to pick up a scent in the snow-laden air. He snuffled along the ground, now covered with white. Then he stopped and snuffled deeply down to the ground. There it was. Human smell. Heading upwind and uphill.

He kept his nose to the ground and followed the hunters' trail. As he determined their direction, he picked up speed. They had what he needed. Food. And with the snow falling, Old Scar Face knew the time for his long sleep was fast approaching. One more good meal and he might make it through this winter. He picked up his speed and began his hunt in earnest.

TWENTY

ELLIE DIDN'T DARE TOUCH the body. She could barely stand to look at it. Even though the face looked familiar, she couldn't remember who it was. Maybe the hit on her head caused her to lose her memory.

The face looked so waxen; it hardly appeared human. She couldn't see the limbs; they were covered with leaves. But she could see the deep open wound in the abdomen and the blood crusted around it and on the shirt. She saw some of the intestines hanging out and more curled inside. She turned away and struggled to her feet.

Buddy stayed next to her, whining softly. He pulled at her pant leg, trying to get her to move.

"All right, Buddy, I'm leaving. But I'm going to tie my scarf around a tree so we can lead Dave back here."

She pulled her red scarf from her face and fastened it to a branch. Then, taking one more glance at the body, she turned, holding her head, and slowly walked in the direction where she thought the cross-country trail was. When they finally pushed through the hemlock bushes to the trail, Ellie bent down, removed Buddy's scarf and tied it to a limb next to the trail.

"There. They'll know where to hunt for it."

Her head still pulsed with every step. She rubbed the back of her head gently. Yes, the egg was still there and it radiated pain so intense every step was agony. However, Ellie kept on walking because she had no choice. No one knew where she was. She didn't have her cell phone. And now as the wind picked up, snow started to spit down out of the dark sky.

Ellie tried to walk faster, but she couldn't. She would have to stop every few moments and rest until her head stopped pounding so hard. Buddy would nudge her and she would start her wobbly walk again.

"Only a mile, Buddy, only one mile. We can make it," Ellie encouraged herself as she plodded along.

She was growing cold and wrapped her arms around herself. She wasn't dressed for snow. Low-cut and not insulated, her hiking boots were more suited for fall weather than winter. Her socks were not wool, rather a new propylene mix that wicked moisture. Better than cotton, she supposed, and walking did help to keep her feet from freezing, unlike her fingers. She started to flex her fingers under her armpits to keep the circulation going as she walked.

The effort to walk uphill on the rugged course was slowly stealing her energy. She stopped frequently. Her rest stops grew longer and her walking time shorter. Buddy pulled at her several times to get her going again.

"Good dog," she whispered. "Keep at me, boy."

The snow fell. Ellie and Buddy's footsteps marked the snow on the ground. Ellie walked with her eyes half-closed, stumbling over snow-covered branches and rocks. She slipped and fell several times and cried out with pain. Each time Buddy would grab her coat with his teeth and pull at her until she got up again and started to walk. She followed him, holding on to his tail, no longer knowing where she was or how long she had walked.

She only knew she wanted to lie down and rest, sleep awhile until her head felt better. Thoughts of sleep obsessed her. Her eyes grew heavier. Finally, she closed them and just let Buddy lead her. Her hand loosened on his tail. She just wanted to lie down in the soft snow with Buddy and sleep until her head didn't hurt anymore.

TWENTY-ONE

ROSIE PULLED OUT her cell phone and speed dialed 2, her code for Colby, again. Nothing. The screen showed the same message, "out of service."

"Damn." Rosie pushed the phone back in her coat pocket and pulled out the two-way. She clicked it on. "Calling Colby. Do you read? Come in, please."

She clicked to receive. Nothing. She called again. "Colby, it's me. Rosie. I'm on the Wilson trail, looking for you. Return my call. Out."

There was no answer. She tried three more times with no results. She called out his name repeatedly. The snow-laden branches muffled her voice. She looked around, hoping to see some sign of him. She walked off trail on both sides, kicking at the snow, scraping snow off rocks, dead logs, anything that might be a body covered with snow.

She was worried. More worried now than she had been earlier. She knew something was wrong. Colby would have called, would have let them know what was going on. If he could. That thought wouldn't leave her. If he could. So, he couldn't. Why not?

Rosie's interest was more than professional. Her concern was more than one colleague for another. Over the months she had worked for the Hummingbird Falls Police Department, she had grown fond of Dave, but she had fallen for Colby, and hard. She kept her feelings hidden, afraid they would bring her all kinds of grief. Not only might she receive an embarrassing rejection from the handsome young officer, but also perhaps a pink slip for inappropriate feelings or behavior toward a fellow worker from her boss, Dave. She feared for the well-being of a colleague, but more so for a man she cared very much about, had come to love. She wiped a cold tear from her eye.

She tried to reach Dave with the cell phone. No service. What should she do? What could she do? Her options were to return to the SUV and call Dave again on the car radiophone, update him and ask him to bring the search dogs. Or she could follow the trail farther, hoping to see some sign of Colby. Then she came up with a third option.

She punched the two-way on and tried to raise the winter crew in the hiking hut farther up the mountain at the top of the trail. She switched to the emergency band.

"Rosie O'Rourke to Wilson Hut. Are you there? Repeat. Wilson hut. Are you receiving?" Static rattled.

Then a voice answered, "Rosie, hi. Stan here. What's up? Over."

"I'm on the Wilson Trail, trying to find Colby Conners. Have you seen or heard from him? Over."

Static again and then more faintly, Stan replied, "Negative, Rosie. Haven't seen or heard from Colby. Storm's fierce up here. He may have stopped at a lean-to or holed up to wait out the weather. Over."

"Thanks. Keep an eye out, will you? If he gets there, have him call me on the two-way. Over."

"Will do. Everything okay? Over."

"I hope so. Seen anyone else? Over."

"No. I'm alone. The trail's officially closed. Hazardous conditions. Should be a notice on the sign-in box by now. Lots of steep slopes, dangerous when wet and icy. Over."

"Could you hike down trail a bit? Check the trail below? See if you see Colby or anyone else? Over."

"Already tried. Could only get a little way. Then sheer ice. No one's going to make it up or down. Whatever you do, don't climb up here. Over."

"I hear you. If anyone shows up, check ID and be careful. Then call me. Got it? Over."

Static crackled. "Can hardly hear you. The wind's blasting. What's happening down there? Over."

"Not sure yet. Keep alert. Might be some trouble headed your way. Maybe some guys from New Jersey who're bad news. Over."

"Rosie, lost…last transmission. Try again. I've…." The two-way hissed with different pitches of scratchy sound.

Rosie tried to reach Stan several more times, but eventually gave up. She stared around her. The snow was falling thick and fast. The wind was blowing the large flakes horizontally and tree trunks were turning white where the snow blasted them. She hiked cautiously down trail to the lot, feeling like she was walking though a gauntlet of ghosts.

She called Colby's name while she walked, and tried to listen for an answer, but her own footsteps and puffing breath hindered her hearing. Finally, she reached the trailhead, pulled a blank sign-up sheet out of the box and wrote in capital letters, TRAIL CLOSED. HAZARDOUS CONDITIONS. She ripped the list of hikers' names off the clipboard, stuffed it in her pocket, and put the warning note on the top of the clipboard, wondering why the ranger assigned to tack up the notices didn't leave one here.

Rosie ran to her SUV, unlocked the door and started the engine and windshield wipers. While she popped on the heater full blast, she picked up the radiophone and called Dave.

"Dave here. You find him?"

"No," Rosie breathed. "And more bad news. I found his hat on the trail. It's smeared with blood. No sign of him."

"No. Are you sure it's his hat? How much blood?"

"It's his, all right. His HFPD red hat. There wasn't much blood on the cap, but obviously he's hurt."

"Colby's sharp. He might have left the cap behind on purpose. See any other signs?"

"No. Conditions are bad; everything's snow covered. I two-wayed Stan, up at the Wilson Hut, but he hasn't seen Colby and the trail's closed now because of hazardous conditions. Colby's got to be between where I found the cap and the hut. I'm afraid he might be hurt. I'm going back up the trail and look some more. We need a rescue crew and search dogs ASAP. Snow's piling up and conditions deteriorating. I think you should give a call to the mountain rescue people, too. Get here as fast as you can. It's snowing like hell and it's freezing cold. Hurry."

TWENTY-TWO

BUDDY BARKED AT ELLIE and tugged at her gloved hand. "Just let me rest a little longer, Buddy. I'm so tired." Ellie lay back in the snow and closed her eyes.

But Buddy wouldn't let her alone. He pushed her with his nose. He licked her face. He growled and bit at her legs.

"Stop, Buddy. Stop."

But Buddy wouldn't stop. He continued to paw at her, bark, lick and try to pull her along the trail.

"Okay, okay. You win. I'll get up. But I'm so cold, Buddy."

Ellie opened her eyes and looked around. The snow was coming down even harder, swirling with the wind gusts. It was hard to see anything, let alone recognize landmarks indicating they were going in the right direction.

"Where are we, Buddy? Home, let's go home." Ellie pushed herself to a sitting position and then, leaning on Buddy, stood up.

Buddy took her glove in his mouth and walked on. He stopped by a tree and barked. Ellie looked up. There was a blue blaze half-hidden by the covering snow.

"Good dog, you found the trail. Now, home, Buddy, home."

Buddy took her glove in his teeth again and tugged Ellie on. Encouraged by the blue blazes they passed,

Ellie gained hope and tried to pick up her pace a bit. However, the pain in her head quickly slowed her back to a stumbling walk.

Twenty minutes later, she heard the sound of water. They were approaching Foster's Brook.

"Oh, Buddy. We're almost there. Only a little way to go. Home, now."

They exited the woods onto the trail by the creek. It was brighter out in the clearing and Ellie's spirits rose.

"Only a few more yards, Buddy."

The turn-off path to Ellie's cabin was up on the right. A familiar cry met them. Seven crows perched on white-tipped trees along the path. They were spaced twenty feet apart, each crow on a separate tree. When Ellie and Buddy walked by a crow-inhabited tree, the bird would caw four times, as Ellie and Buddy passed its position. Seven crows, twenty-eight caws. Ellie looked up. She could barely see the black crows in the white blizzard. Their cries were welcoming, but eerie as well.

As Ellie and Buddy approached the newly replaced bird feeders in the backyard, two crows swooped down, flew over the tired trekkers and landed on a feeder. The bird feeder tilted and seeds slid onto the snow. The other five crows flocked down and started to feed voraciously as the two who provided the seeds took guard positions back up on the top of a tree.

Ellie nodded her head at the crows, less convinced now they belonged at the top of her list of suspected vandals who had destroyed her bird feeders earlier this fall. Dave and folks at the Pastry Shop insisted bears were guilty of destroying her feeders as they attempted to fatten up for hibernation.

Most locals didn't fill their bird feeders during the fall, waiting until hibernation was underway. The same was true in the early spring when bears coming out of hibernation were starving and anxious to eat anything they could find. Bird feeders were not put out and filled until enough greens and insects existed to satisfy the bears' hunger. Villagers were cautious about drawing bears closer to civilization with food. They knew better than to addict the bears to handouts. Bears enjoyed a longer life span if they stayed wild and suspicious of humans.

Ellie countered the locals' opinion about bears robbing her feeders with skepticism. She hadn't seen any signs of bears around her new cabin. True, last year at the cottage she rented, a bear broke into her kitchen one night after smelling the blueberry turnovers sitting out on the kitchen table. But Ellie still wasn't convinced her vandal this fall was a bear.

Stubborn her whole life, Ellie wanted to hold on to her belief the crows she had seen pecking at the feeders, keeping the smaller birds at bay, were the culprits. She remembered reading they were crafty critters, able to make and use tools. They could sharpen twigs to forage for insects and larvae; they even could adjust the size of the twig if needed. She had seen them place acorns and beechnuts on the road and wait for a car to pass by and crack them open. Now they were demonstrating for her how they could get all the seeds they wanted from her feeders. However, she observed, they stole those seeds without damaging the feeders. Maybe a bear did the harm after all.

She started to shake her head at the thought, then stopped because of the pain. She and Buddy started walking again, stumbling through the snow to the screened back porch. Without kicking off her snowy boots, Ellie opened the back door and entered the warm cabin. Her woodstove was still burning and she added several pieces of wood to it before she sat down.

Then she slumped down on the couch in front of the fire, fully dressed, leaned her head back and closed her eyes. She was so tired and her head seemed to hurt more than ever. Buddy jumped up beside her and put his muzzle in her lap.

Ellie hugged him. "You're the best dog, ever. You saved my life, Buddy. Thank you. Thank God we're back safely."

Then she remembered what she had seen in the woods. The dead body. She forced herself to get up and grab the phone. She eased back down on the couch and called the Hummingbird Falls police station.

TWENTY-THREE

"HELLO. HUMMINGBIRD FALLS Police. How may I help you? This's Betsy Walker, dispatch, speaking."

"Betsy, this is Ellie Hastings, up at Foster's Brook. Is Dave there? It's an emergency."

"Hi, Ellie. I'm sorry, Dave's out. Can I help you?"

"I don't know. I was out walking this morning, before the snow started. I got knocked out and when I woke up there was a body—a dead body—a few yards away. I think it might be someone I know; only I can't remember his name. Somebody needs to get up here and get him."

"Ellie, could you repeat that, please? You're talking so fast, all the words blurred together. I don't know if I heard you right. You were knocked out? Right? Do you know who knocked you out? Are you safe? Is the perpetrator still there? Do you need an ambulance?"

"Yes and no. Yes, I was knocked out and no, I don't know who did it. I'm safe now and I don't need an ambulance. But the important thing I'm trying to tell you is there's someone dead out there. On the cross-country trail. The one from Coldwater to Foster's Brook. The one with the blue blazes."

"You don't need an ambulance? You're sure? You don't sound so good. I could send one up."

"No, Betsy. Don't send an ambulance. Did you hear me say there's a dead body?"

"Yes, I did, Ellie. Now exactly where is the body?"

"I'm not sure. But I tied a red scarf on a branch next to the trail where I cut into the woods when I was running after Buddy. He actually found the body. I only noticed it after I came to. I tied another scarf near the body, up high, where Dave could find it."

"All right. Hold on for a minute, Ellie. I'm calling the fire department."

"Wait," Ellie yelled. "I don't need the fire department."

But it was already too late. She was on hold. So Ellie held, laying her aching head back on the couch. Buddy finished licking off his wet feet and was lapping up water from his bowl.

A minute later, Betsy's voice came on the phone. "Ellie, are you still there? I've notified the fire chief of the situation. He's put out a call to the coroner and the volunteer crew to meet at the fire station. They're going to go up and look for the body."

"Why did you call them? Where're Dave, Rosie and Colby?"

"Everyone's gone, Ellie. The next in command is Howie Holmes, the fire chief. Could you repeat the co-ordinates of where you found the body, please?"

Ellie tried to explain where she saw the body. After repeating the information about four more times, Betsy was finally satisfied and said she would relay the information to Howie.

"Now Ellie, are you sure you're okay? You don't want a doctor or the paramedics to come up and check you out? I think you should have someone with you."

"No, Betsy. But thanks. I'm just too tired now to

think about it." Ellie hung up the phone, exhausted. She struggled out of her orange vest, coat, boots and extra layers. She just dropped everything on the floor and then pushed herself up off the couch and headed for the kitchen. She put the kettle on for tea and rummaged in the refrigerator and cupboards for some quick energy snack.

"Darn, I forgot I threw them all away when I started this stupid diet. What I really need now is a blueberry turnover."

Ellie sank down on the old pine kitchen chair, her aching head in her hands, and waited for the kettle to boil. Buddy came into the kitchen and looked up at her. She pushed herself off the chair and got his dog biscuits.

Organic and homemade, entrepreneur-in-the-making Henry, age eleven, of Hummingbird Falls, created these natural biscuits. He sold them every Saturday at the Hummingbird Falls Farmers Market. Ellie made sure to buy a small bag of biscuits from handsome Henry, who would entertain her with his fantastic imagination. The two swapped stories and laughs. Whether the tales were invented or real, she could never tell, and Henry never told either. She gave Buddy two biscuits, sank back into her chair and watched him wolf them down.

"Why not?" she asked as she looked at the packaging. "Says 'perfectly safe for humans, too.'"

Ellie picked up a biscuit, looked it over, and then took a nibble. Buddy looked at her, his head cocked to one side. She took another bite.

"Hmm. Not bad. I can taste the peanut butter, I think. Maybe a little crispy, but a dunk in a teaspoon of honey might help. Actually, it's kind of tasty. Thanks, Henry. Just what I needed."

She pulled some more biscuits out of the package. She dipped one into the honey pot sitting in the center of the kitchen table and nibbled on it. She gave Buddy two more. By the time she finished her second biscuit, the teakettle was whistling and she brewed up a big pot of raspberry tea. She dropped two teaspoons of honey in her mug while the pot brewed.

"Just to get my energy back," she explained to Buddy.

Her phone rang. She poured hot tea into her mug, took it with her into the living room and sank down on the couch. What now? She picked up the phone.

TWENTY-FOUR

DAVE LEFT THE OFFICE long before Ellie called about finding the body. He stopped at the town garage and found Larry putting the plows on the dark green Hummingbird Falls dump trucks.

"I need you. Colby's in trouble up at Wilson's trail."

Larry looked up, holding a wrench in his greasy hand.

"What kinda trouble? I got thirty-five miles of roads need plowing and I got caught without my plows on."

"Big trouble, I'm afraid. Can't you call your crew to get these trucks ready?"

"Well, I could, but Fred's sick with flu, Sam's wife just had another baby and he's needed at home, and Bobby doesn't know how to put the plows on. So, I'm stuck. What about Howie?"

"I don't want to call him unless I really have to. Folks'll be lighting up their stoves and fireplaces with this cold and snow. I'm sure we'll have six or more alarms for chimney fires. Always happens first big snowfall. And Howie doesn't have enough volunteers as it is."

"What about Mike? Or Reggie at the deli? Maybe James at the Foster's Home for Children. They could help."

"They'll do. Thanks for the suggestions, Larry. I always come to you first 'cause I've deputized you so many times and you know how to handle emergencies."

"You saying Colby's in an emergency?"

"I don't know, yet, but it sure looks like it. Rosie's up on Wilson's trail trying to track him down. Found his hat on the trail. Some blood on it. Doesn't look good."

"Doesn't sound good, either. Here, use my phone. Call Mike, James and Reggie. I'll use my cell and call a few of the guys who hang out down at Tomorrow's. See if they can help."

The two men made phone calls, watching out the window at the wind-driven snow. Although still passable, at the rate the snow was falling the mountain roads would soon become dangerous.

"That settles it for me," Larry said. "Superintendent's closing the school early. I've got to get the plows out before the school buses pick up the kids. All the guys down at Tomorrow's are part-time drivers and have to report. So you'll have to find someone else."

"I called the AMC rescue guys and they're calling their volunteers. Mike's meeting me down here in a few minutes. Reggie's chasing his last customers out and closing up and will join us. We'll pick James up on the way. So, I should be all set for now. That's one of the great things about a small village like ours. Everyone helps out in an emergency."

"Sorry I can't go with you, Dave. I've climbed Wilson's trail every year and know it by heart. It's tricky. Not as bad as Harrington's Ridge or Tollerman's, but almost. Be careful up there. I imagine the trail's closed higher up. Those ridges get iced up bad."

"Doesn't matter. If an officer of mine's up there in

trouble, I'm going up, no matter how bad it is. Thanks for the warning, though. I haven't climbed the mountain for years. I had a hard enough time then. As I remember there're some pretty sharp up-and-down cliffs, with almost no footing."

"You're right. And when it's wet or icy, forget it. You really shouldn't go up at all in this weather."

"I heard you, Larry. But I gotta go."

"Here, take my hiking sticks and ice cleats. They might help a little. I got some climbing ropes, too." Mike bundled the cleats, rope, an ice axe and some pinions into a canvas bag.

"Thanks. There's Mike now. Be careful on the roads, Larry. I'm glad we have a man like you in charge."

"You be careful, too. We need you around here, guy."

The two men hugged and then Dave banged out the garage door into the whipping snow. Mike gestured for Dave to jump into his big Chevy four-wheel-drive truck. Dave was driving his own Subaru; both of the Hummingbird Falls official vehicles were in use. Dave saw two big crates in the back of Mike's truck.

"Thanks for bringing the dogs. I hope we don't need them, but it's a comfort knowing if we do, they're here."

"No, problem. They need the exercise and practice anyway."

Mike swung through town, picked up Reggie and then headed up the Falls Road to get James. He pushed the truck into four-wheel drive as he started skidding on the icy road.

"Starting to freeze up. This could be quite a thrilling ride. Hold on."

Reggie and Dave grabbed the side straps and followed Mike's instruction.

"Take it easy, Mike. We don't want to have an accident. It would only add another problem to the one we have," Dave said. "And it wouldn't help Colby or Rosie at all. So slow and easy does it."

"Okay. But if anybody's hurts my buddy Colby or touches a red hair on Rosie's head, they'll have me to deal with," Mike said as he turned out of a skid. "I'll hunt 'em down and skin 'em."

"Don't make me sorry I asked you to help, Mike. We don't know what we're getting into here. Hopefully, it's nothing."

"Have you heard from Rosie?"

"Not since I talked to her on the car phone about forty-five minutes ago. Cells don't work up there. I have my two-way with me, but it's out of range until we get closer."

"She's a tough gal," said Reggie. "She'll take care of herself."

"Yep," said Dave. "She's a good one. But we don't know what she's up against either. And she's hunting for Colby all by herself right now. That's not good."

TWENTY-FIVE

THE SQUALL WAS BLOWING snow full force. As Rosie trudged through the drifts, she was sure the word *blizzard* was a more accurate description of what was happening around her. The wind was relentless now, driving the snow sideways right into her face. She pulled her scarf up over her nose and wished she had brought goggles to protect her eyes. As she started up the trail, she could see no more than a few feet in front of her. How was she ever going to find Colby if he had strayed or been pulled off the trail?

Rosie decided to stay on the trail as long as she could. If she had to turn back, then she would hike off trail and search to the left and right of the trail as she traveled down. She made some progress on the first mile where the trail slowly rose and was dirt-packed under the snow. As the path grew steeper, she had to traverse more boulders and small ice-covered brooks. She tried to jump the brooks or seek stepping-stones across, afraid of getting her boots and feet wet. Wet feet in this weather spelled disaster.

As Rosie made her way around a U-turn in the trail, she came upon a clearing. She remembered last year's ice storm destroyed most of the white birches in this area. The blowdowns lay like pick-up sticks, covered in vanilla frosting and piled in complete disorder. The clearing looked impossible to move through. Rosie floundered up the trail as it wound its way back and forth and around the broken trunks as it continued up the mountain. Often, she would have to scale an icy snow-mounded pile of logs to find the trail on the other side.

She scanned the stacks of deadwood, looking for any sign of color, since identifying shapes was impossible in the whiteout conditions. She figured Colby would be in his black leather fleece-lined police jacket, similar to hers. The black should stand out against the white bark of the birches and white snow background. Every time she thought she saw something shaped like a man, her heart beat wildly, hoping it might be Colby. However, the object always turned out to be a rock sticking out of the snow or a partially hidden log.

Once she saw a group of crows, huddled together on the top of a heap of derelict trunks. She shuddered. The crows sat like black-robed judges in a white courtroom, about to pronounce a death sentence.

In defiance, Rosie yelled at the crows, "Fly away. Get out of here. Do some good. Go find Colby." The crows only flapped snow off their wings and continued to stare at her.

Leaving the clearing behind, Rosie entered the dark spruce-and-fir forest again. She still had a long way to go on the trail before hitting the timberline, where only scrub brush and alpine wild flowers grew in the warmer months. Snow would have buried all signs of these hardy plants long before she got there.

In the woods, the trees blocked the sharp wind a bit and Rosie decided to stop, hydrate with a drink of her energy water and eat a high-protein bar. Climbing at this altitude reduced her oxygen intake, dehydrated her body and drained her energy. She knew if she didn't take care of herself properly, she would be unable to continue very much farther.

As she leaned against a maple tree, munching her bar and drinking water, she looked around. She couldn't see very far in the heavy snow, and what she did see wasn't comforting. She realized at least one foot of snow had fallen this high up on the mountain and where the wind had blown the snow into drifts it mounded as high as her waist. The snow would deepen even more as she ascended.

What if she did find Colby, injured? How would she transport him down the trail? She cursed when she realized she forgot to bring the expandable sled. She didn't want to imagine having to use the sled, or that Colby might be hurt so badly he would need it.

Maybe Colby didn't climb all the way up the trail. Maybe he turned around and went back down, forgetting or for some other reason not signing out at the trailhead. Maybe someone forced him into a car in the parking lot, drove him away and he never climbed the trail at all. He could have dropped his hat on the way down, not on the way up, as she was assuming.

Other ugly thoughts swarmed in her brain. What if someone hurt him and hid his body? She felt staggered. She would never find him then. If he were somewhere out in the woods, she was just wasting time with this climb. He might still be alive and she could be moving farther and farther away from him while he lay hurt, needing help.

Frantic, she tried the cell phone and two-way again. Nothing but static on the two-way. No service on the cell and the batteries were almost dead. She clicked the phone off, to preserve what little battery strength remained.

What else could she do? She finished her bar, no longer tasting it, secured the water in her pack and started to climb again. Her progress from here up was going to be tedious and slow. The snow-covered trail rose steeply before her. The trees were thinning out. The wind could attack her with its full force now.

She pushed against the strength of the blasting wind and pulled her legs up through the foot or more of snow. With each step, she grew more exhausted; her breath was ragged and she realized she was panting for oxygen. She had to stop more often just to stop her heart from racing so fast. Her legs burned with every step.

When she paused to take another drink of water, she raised her eyes and saw what she had been looking for and dreading. A six-foot-long mound of snow lay across the trail ahead. She dropped the water bottle and stumbled forward as fast as she could. She fell to her knees and started scraping away the snow. Black boots. Just like Colby's. Winter wool hiking pants, black like Colby wore. A black leather jacket zipped up the front and covered with a neon orange hunter's vest. She reached to brush the snow from the face. She screamed and covered her face with her hands.

TWENTY-SIX

THE THREE HUNTERS stopped pushing through the snow and huddled together, rubbing their hands and stamping their feet.

"This isn't doing us any good," Jim yelled above the wind. "Admit it, we're lost. We've been going downhill for over an hour and haven't seen any sign of a trail."

"But we're going downhill, at least. We have to come out at the bottom, right?" asked Andy.

"Not necessarily so," Bob puffed. "I remember the map showed some topography going downhill and ending up in swamps. We could be working our way even farther into the wilderness without knowing it."

"What'll we do? What're we supposed to do if we're lost?" asked Jim.

"Stay where we are, I guess. Unless we know which way to go, we could just end up farther and farther away in the wrong direction. Maybe we should wait out the storm here. Make a shelter and a fire and wait for someone to come after us," Bob said.

"And how long do we wait?" Jim complained. "No one in their right mind would come out in this weather. No one knows where we're hunting. No one expects us back. The motel manager sure ain't going to call anybody if we aren't there before he goes to bed. Nobody'll find us. We'll freeze to death right here."

"Calm down. We're not dead yet and we're not going to be. The snow'll stop. Some other hunters will come along. One night isn't going to hurt us," Bob said.

"Oh, yeah? We could freeze to death out here. I'm cold, really cold, too cold. I think it's a good idea to build a fire, but after we eat something and get warmed up, I think we should keep going. It'll be pitch-dark soon. I don't want to spend the night lost in the woods."

"Maybe your survivor book has some answers," Andy said.

"Don't start with me, man, not now."

"No. I'm serious. It's like serendipitous stuff, isn't it? We get stuck in a snowstorm and get lost and you just happen to have a book on surviving. When we get back we could write a book about how that stinking library book saved us from certain death. We'd make millions. Maybe what seems bad here is really the best luck we could have."

"I think you're going nuts; that's what I think. Shut up and look for someplace for us to get some shelter from this storm."

"Okay, Jim. Just trying to lighten things up, just talking, that's all. No offense intended."

Bob was trying to see through the blowing snow. "What about under those fir trees? Snow's covered the branches and underneath might be clear and dry."

The three men trudged over to the massive hemlock. Its limbs bent down to the ground with their heavy load of snow. As they crawled under into the dark interior, they snapped on their flashlights and scanned the area. They could see brown leaves and sticks carpeting the ground and only a sprinkling of snow.

"Jackpot!" Jim yelled. "Just what we need. Hardly

any snow in here and we can scrape up this dry stuff in no time."

He threw off his pack and kneeled on the ground. He scrabbled around piling up kindling. Bob took out his lighter and tried to ignite the pile Jim gathered.

"No good. They aren't catching. Maybe they're rotten or too damp. We need really dry stuff."

"Good luck, Dumbo. Just where do you think we're going to find dry material?" Jim stared at Bob, his mouth twisted into a sneer.

Andy was busy ruffling through his pockets and day pack. He managed to gather a couple of receipts and a checkbook.

"Here's some dry paper," he said.

"Good idea. Let me see what I've got," Bob said.

He stood up and went through his pack and pockets and Jim searched his pockets and day pack as well. They each contributed some pieces of paper to the pile.

"Wait. Before you light it, let's get more kindling and some logs," Andy said. "We can stack them under here to keep them clear of the snow."

The three men stumbled back out into the blizzard, looking for firewood. Snow covered everything. The hunters stamped around, using their feet to locate a branch or log. They scraped the snow off and then grappled the pieces out of the icy-hard frosted ground. They were sweating by the time they regrouped under the hemlock with their loads. They shook off as much snow as possible before stacking the wood and kindling next to the tree trunk.

"Now, let's pick the driest wood, the smallest pieces, and pile them with the paper we have. Then I'll try to light it. It should catch now," Bob said.

The three men searched through the wood, selecting the driest pieces. Bob knelt down again, arranged the leaves and little sticks in a tent shape with the pieces of paper inside. He placed a bigger stick on top of the kindling tent and held his lighter to the pieces of paper they had contributed from their pockets.

"Hoorah!" A shout of glee and a round of backslapping and high fives accompanied the little flame consuming the paper goods and sending small sparks onto the sticks.

"Oh, no!" Groans followed as the small fire sputtered out, doused by the wind and the wet wood.

"What now, great leader?" Jim growled. "All our paper's gone. The wood's too wet. We're soaked from tramping around getting wood which won't burn. I'm even colder than before. At least walking kept my blood moving around."

"Will you shut up? You're driving me bonkers with your whining. If you remember, you wanted to start a fire. Why don't you try your hand at it, wise guy?" Bob shot back.

Andy came to the rescue. "What about your survivor book, Jim? Get it out of your pack. We can read about how to start a fire with wet wood and then use the pages to start the fire."

"While you're at it, Jim, pull out the extra clothes you have in there. The more layers we have on, the warmer we'll be," Bob added.

Jim looked at Bob and Andy. "I'm willing to donate my library book to the fire, but you guys have to pay the library fine."

Andy and Bob stared at him in disbelief. "How can you worry about a library fee when we're stuck out here in a blizzard? Dude, you're unbelievable."

"Just thought I'd mention it," Jim mumbled. He opened his pack and pulled out clothes. Most of them were wet and stuck together with icy snow. He retrieved the book and closed his backpack up quickly. He handed the book to Bob.

"It's soaking wet."

"Okay, so I didn't shake the snow off my stuff when I put it back in my pack. Big deal. How could I know you'd want to use the book to light a fire? Do you think the pages are too wet to burn?"

"Probably. But we can look up how to get a fire going anyway." Bob turned the pages. "Andy, shine your flashlight over here. It's too dark to read under this tree."

The three men huddled closely together in the shelter under the huge hemlock. Andy sat on one side of Bob, holding the flashlight; Jim, on the other side, leaned in and bent over trying to read as Bob thumbed though the wadded pages looking for directions on how to light a fire with wet wood.

Outside the hemlock, the wind continued to howl and the heavy snow piled up deeper and deeper. As the snow drifted, all evidence of the three men disappeared. It was if they had never been there at all.

TWENTY-SEVEN

THE THREE HUNTERS BENT over the small fire, holding their hands as close as they dared to the little flames. After numerous attempts to follow the survivor book's directions on how to light a fire with wet wood, they finally succeeded.

They used the driest of the library book's pages, curled tightly. They placed pine needles, small shavings stripped off dead fir branches with their Swiss Army knives and tiny twigs in the pile. They huddled together closely, blocking as much wind as possible before Andy struck a match and set the matchbook on fire. At the same time, Bob attacked the small pile of kindling with his lighter. The additional heat did the trick. As the shavings caught, the men quickly whittled more. Then as the fire gained strength, they added bigger twigs and small branches. Although the fire sputtered and almost went out a few times, soon it was hot enough to dry out the small twigs and ignite them.

"My hands are finally warming up. I wish my feet would; they feel like blocks of ice. I'm not sure I can move my toes," Bob said.

"How about we put some cheese and crackers over the fire? We could mix them up into a kind of stew. I'm starved and I think we should keep our stamina up,"

Andy responded. "Hot food might help warm our blood and thaw out our insides and feet."

"I don't know if it works that way, but good idea about trying to warm up some food. The cheese'll melt and we can throw some trail mix in with it," said Bob.

"How about throwing the leftover bacon on?" Jim asked.

"Leftover bacon? I packed it up at breakfast. It's in my pack, back where we ate this morning."

"Well, I kinda unpacked it and stowed it in my backpack while you guys were trying to figure out how to rope them up. I've got it here."

"Damn you, Jim. You stole our bacon? What else did you take?"

"Look. Whatever I took, it's turned out to be a good thing, hasn't it? You should be kissing my feet for taking it and carrying it all this way. After all, I didn't have to tell you, did I?"

Jim looked at Andy's and Bob's faces. Firelight flickered on them, but didn't hide the scowls.

"Of course, I was going to share it with you guys. I was going to surprise you. I figured we'd get hungry, so I just took some of the food along. Come on, guys. Lighten up. At least we won't go hungry."

Andy looked at Bob. Bob stared back. A moment of silence hung in the icy air.

"We could kill you for the food, you know, Jim. We might even eat you, like they did in the Alps when the plane carrying the soccer team went down," Bob threatened.

"Or like at Donner Pass when the pioneers got stuck for months one winter," added Andy. "They had to eat each other to survive."

Jim's mouth froze in a wide O.

Then Andy and Bob started to laugh. They banged Jim on the arms and back, gasping in hysterical laughter.

"Jim, you've probably saved our lives. Thanks, man."

"Good thinking. What've you got? Pull it all out."

Jim relaxed and started to laugh, too. "You would eat me if I didn't have food? Really?"

"Not me," Andy cried through his laughs. "I don't need food that much."

Jim began taking out the food he had stashed in his backpack. Cheese, hotdogs, bacon, a couple of potatoes, a package of macaroni and cheese, two freeze-dried beef stew dinner packages, packets of dried soup and a package of chocolate-chip cookies.

"I think that's all of it."

"Man, it looks good. All we need is a pan to cook in and we're set."

"Oh, no. Watch the fire. It's going out."

The three men carefully bent back over the dying fire and Bob blew gently on it while Andy and Jim fed it shavings and more twigs.

"We have to build this up bigger if we want it to last," said Bob. "Before we cook anything, let's stockpile some shavings, roll up the rest of the pages from the book and load up on small twigs and branches. We'll have to keep tending it until it's strong enough to take logs. Then, we shouldn't have to watch it so carefully."

The three men bent to the task. The lure of hot water and food drove them to work as fast as cold fingers and stiff muscles let them. Gradually, warmth grew inside the cover of the hemlock branches and little drops of melted snow started falling from overhead.

"It's hot enough now," Bob said. "We can put the potatoes in the coals and heat water in whatever we can find."

"I've got a camp kit. I've had it since I was a Boy Scout. It all fits together: a cup and pan which doubles as a plate," said Andy as he took a tin contraption off his equipment belt.

"Just what we need. Great. We've got it all. Cook the hot dogs and bacon on sticks over the fire and we'll warm water and throw in the stew and soup in the pan. We even have desert." The men set to cooking their dinner in high spirits.

"Sure smells good," Bob said as the hot dogs singed and the bacon dripped fat into the fire.

The smoke rose through the lower branches and blew downwind carrying the scent of food with it. The smell of cooking food drifted toward Old Scar Face as he made his way through the snow on the hunt for his next meal.

TWENTY-EIGHT

OLD SCAR FACE DIDN'T mind the snow. His wide paws worked like snowshoes and his long claws gave him good purchase on the icy spots. Occasionally, he would stop for a minute to shake his body, flinging matted snow in a circle around him before plodding onward. He knew he was coming closer, gaining on the humans. The body scent was stronger.

Old Scar Face was ravenous. He focused on one thing only: finding food to fill his stomach. Right now, the food he was after was with the humans he hunted. He picked up his pace and moved on across the mountain after them.

In a short while, he lifted his head. Snuffling, he rose up on his hind legs and turned slowly in a circle. Fire. Food. Close by.

Old Scar Face made a sound deep in his throat. It could have been a groan of relief, a prayer, or a sound of determination. Then he started to lope though the deep snow toward the delicious smells whipping toward him in the icy air.

TWENTY-NINE

HOWIE, THE HUMMINGBIRD Falls fire chief and only paid firefighter, managed to contact his most reliable and available village volunteers: plumber Paul Hays, electrician Bill Gunter, Simon White, owner of the Look Out Inn, engineer Chen Ey and farmer Wendy Hill. Doc Muller, the only doctor in Hummingbird Falls, who served as the county coroner, also agreed to meet them at the fire station in the village.

Howie welcomed his crew with, "Ellie Hastings called in and reported she found a dead body up near the Jefferson Trail this morning, just before the blizzard roared in. Since Dave, Colby and Rosie are working a case up the notch, we've been authorized to find the body and secure the crime scene until they're available."

Paul started asking questions, one right after the other.

"Hold on, Paul. One thing at a time. Ellie didn't know who the dead person was. She evidently thought he looked familiar, but she had fallen, hit her head and was unconscious for a while, so who knows how the shock affected her. So, we don't know who we're looking for."

Howie turned from putting blankets into the back of the emergency vehicle and answered Paul's next question. "Look, I don't know exactly where the body is. Ellie left a couple of red scarves on the old Jefferson cross-country ski trail, so we'll have to hike up there and find them. Hopefully, they didn't blow away in this wind."

Doc Muller asked, "Can the rescue truck make it up the mountain? Snow's accumulating fast. I had a little trouble just making it over here."

"This truck's specially equipped for the mountains and all of us can squeeze in, two in front and the rest in the back. We need enough people to carry out the body. It could be a tough recovery. That trail hasn't been groomed in years. I don't imagine it's in very good condition."

Chen asked, "Why not take snowmobiles? Using them would be easier than walking and we could tow the body back on a sled."

"Three reasons I can think of, Chen. First, we can't fit a snowmobile in the emergency truck and there's no tow bar to hook up a trailer. Second, a snowmobile might mark up any clues or footsteps around the crime scene. We'd lose valuable evidence. We have better control if we walk. Three, I don't want risk taking any more vehicles up there than I have to."

The others nodded in agreement.

Wendy suggested, "We could take our skis in the truck. It's faster to ski than walk."

"Good idea, but we don't have the time to pick up everyone's skis and we could have problems skiing that old trail. Frankly, I haven't done much skiing lately. Pulling the sled could be tricky, too, especially if we're on skis. I do have several sets of snowshoes. Anyone who wants to can use those."

Simon and Chen nodded their heads in agreement.

Simon said, "Then, it's settled. We drive up in the

rescue truck, hike up the trail, look for the scarves and carry the body out?"

Doc Muller broke in. "We might have to leave the body there. It all depends on what we find. Dave may want to see it, just like we find it."

Wendy said, "I have a good camera with me. I could take pictures of the scene. Doc, you could take pictures of the body. Then, even if this weather continues, we'd have a good recording of the state of the body when we found it. Dave wouldn't have to travel up there if the blizzard keeps up. The scene could be buried again by then anyway."

"Great thinking, Wendy. Anyone else? No? Then let's get going. The longer we wait, the deeper the snow gets."

"Wow, this's just like in the books I read," Paul said. "Body recovery is a science. We should wear booties over our boots and latex gloves. We'd better keep our eyes open for anything that doesn't look right. Look for evidence. I wish Ellie were here. We should ask her questions, since she's the one who found the body. How did she know where the body was? Maybe she saw something. Sometimes people see things, but don't know it until they're questioned. I've read a lot of mysteries. I've learned a lot about how to solve a crime. We need to…"

"Paul, Paul, stop. Stop. You're moving too fast. We're not crime solvers or forensic techs. We don't even know if there was a crime," said Simon. "We're just going up there to find the body and bring it back."

"Oh, yeah," said Paul.

"Don't look so down, Paul. At least you'll have a good story to tell. How many people around here have found a dead body in a blizzard and hauled it out of the woods? Everyone will know you were part of the recovery team. Why, I'll probably write an article about this for John to print in the paper," Simon added.

Paul brightened and put on his hat. "Thanks, Simon. Maybe we can hit the Pastry Shop after we get back and let everyone know what happened. Let's go."

The volunteers lined up to climb in the back of the truck, throwing their gear in and chatting.

"Just a minute, everyone," said Howie. "I know all the unexpected snow and having this emergency come up is exciting. But don't lose sight of what we're doing. We're hunting for a body. We don't know who. It could be an out-of-state hunter or it could be one of our friends or neighbors. It could be years old or maybe just a day. I don't have to tell you to be prepared for anything. And remember, whoever this was, he had a mother, maybe a brother or sister, could even have had a child."

Howie's speech silenced the volunteers. Initially the adrenaline produced by the emergency call had aroused their anxiety and created a kind of hyper-energy firefighters count on when fighting a fire. But Howie's words brought them back to reality. They weren't rushing off to fight a chimney or brush fire. They were on the hunt for a corpse. And the corpse could be one of their fellow villagers.

THIRTY

ELLIE ANSWERED THE PHONE. "Ellie. It's me. Sarah. Are you okay? Betsy called me and said you were hurt."

The postmistress's voice shook with concern. She and Ellie had been close friends for years. They had even solved some mysteries together.

"Yes, I'm okay, I think. I have a wicked headache and feel a little sick to my stomach. But it could be worse."

"What do you mean it could be worse? What happened? Betsy said you hit your head. Maybe someone attacked you. She said you sounded somewhat funny on the phone. She thinks you might have a concussion."

"Oh, pshaw. I was out walking and something, or maybe someone, whacked me from behind. I fell down and hit my head on a rock. I was unconscious for a while. I don't know how long. And it could be worse because when I woke up I found a dead body. Being dead's a lot worse."

"Oh, my God, a dead body? Who?"

"I don't know. I think I recognized him, but somehow I can't remember."

"You have to see a doctor. It sounds like your brain isn't working. Now. Right away."

"No, no. I'll be fine. I just need to take a nap. I'm so sleepy."

"Ellie. You stop being so foolish and so darn independent. You could be seriously hurt. I can't leave the post office until closing, you know 'neither rain nor snow,' but I'm calling Bonnie, Margaret and Millie. They'll come up and take care of you."

"No, Sarah, it's snowing so hard and the roads are dangerous. I don't want anyone driving up here in this weather. I'll be just fine. Besides, I just want to get in bed and sleep."

"No. Don't go to sleep. You have to stay awake for at least four hours to be sure you don't have a serious injury. At least that's what I think I heard in my first-aid class. I'm not listening to your excuses. Would you rather I called the ambulance and sent them?"

"No. Why're you pestering me? You're making my head hurt even more."

"That does it. Someone will be up to get you and bring you to the doctor within the hour. I don't care whether you want to or not. So just sit where you are and wait. Don't move around and don't take any aspirin. Let your friends help you."

Ellie didn't have the strength to fight. "You win, Sarah. I guess maybe I do need some help right now. I keep getting woozy. Thanks."

Ellie lay down on the couch and closed her eyes. She didn't want to travel downhill in this storm and wait in an emergency room or at the doctor's office. She just wanted to close her eyes and sleep. But her head hurt so much and it didn't seem to be getting any better. What if she did have a concussion? What if she passed out again and no one fed Buddy? Who would take care of him?

Using Buddy as an excuse permitted Ellie to give in

and allow her friends to take care of her. She thought about Alice and Josie, two friends murdered last year. Determined to help her friends and protect the residents in her sweet mountain village, she had worked to uncover the mystery of their deaths and found their murderer. Now Ellie's friends wanted to help her. That's what friends were for, although it was easier for Ellie to help than be helped.

Thinking of good friends, curled up with Buddy on her legs, she fought sleep as long as she could. Finally, the effort to stay awake and the pain of her headache overcame her. Ellie closed her eyes and fell into a deep sleep.

THIRTY-ONE

ROSIE BENT OVER the man's face. She stared at it, trying to find any sign proving her worst nightmare false. A gunshot had blown the right side of the man's face away. Blood covered the left side. Rosie couldn't see the facial features clearly. She prayed it wasn't Colby. She wiped some of the blood off the left side of the face.

It wasn't there.

The little mole she teased Colby about, calling it his beauty mark, wasn't there, under the left eye. Relieved, but needing more evidence, she examined the tip of the victim's left ear lobe. No hole. No sign someone had pierced this ear. When Colby was a wild teenager, he had his left ear pierced and wore a diamond stud. Although he hadn't worn an ear stud for years, a visible dent from the piercing remained.

As Rosie picked out other features, which eliminated Colby as the dead man, she started to relax. This body was not his. But whose body was it? And where was Colby?

Rosie stood up and took the two-way off her belt to get to her baton. She pulled it out to its fullest length and stuck it in the snow piled next to the body. If the snow kept up, it might be hard to find the body later. She tied a small piece of crime scene tape, ripped off when she was securing the truck in the parking lot, onto the baton. It fluttered wildly in the wind.

Rosie was scared. Colby was missing, leaving no message, only a bloody hat behind. Someone had flung blood-covered clothes in the backseat of a truck parked in the lot at the trailhead. Now there was a body with half its face blown off. What would she find next? Or who might find her? It was clear someone besides Colby hiked up this trail before her. She guessed Colby hadn't shot this man. He would have marked the body or hiked back into a cell zone and called.

So, someone else was up here. Rosie looked around, trying to see through the blinding snow. She unzipped her jacket so she could reach her gun more easily. Where was Colby?

Rosie had faced tough situations before. However, this was the first time someone she loved, as a colleague, a friend, and even more, was in such a dangerous situation. Not only was she the lead officer on this search, the one responsible, she was the only one who could do anything to resolve it now. Dave's help might come too late.

She felt pressured and anxious. If she didn't take the right action, Colby's might be the next body she found. But what was the thing to do?

Again, the only thing Rosie could think of was to continue. Keep moving up the trail. Keep looking for Colby. Watch her back. Move with caution. Watch out for whoever was up here with a gun. Someone definitely hiked up here and shot a man to death. To keep alive, she would have to rely on her instinct, training and good common sense. She prayed Dave would get here soon.

Rosie continued walking. Fueled by additional adrenaline, she no longer felt the cold wind or the sting of snow on her face. Her eyes moved right, left, forward. She turned frequently to check behind. She was alert. She watched for any sign that someone was tromping through the snow in front of her.

Visibility was so limited Rosie could see only a few feet in front of or behind her. She tried to compensate by lifting her earflaps and using her hearing. She heard the wind whine through the trees and shriek around the sharp granite ledges. She heard thumping as the wind blew snow clumps off branches to the ground. She heard her own breath whooshing in and out as she struggled up the steep mountain trail. Far away, she heard the cawing of crows. She listened to her footsteps plunge into the snow and pull back out again. She heard the ping of snow as it hit her leather jacket. She heard her heart thumping wildly in her chest.

She listened as she trudged higher and higher. She concentrated on every sound as she stopped for a water break. She was just putting her water bottle back in her pack when she thought she heard a different noise. She paused. It was just what she had been waiting for. She cupped a hand around her ears.

She heard voices. The sound of voices came from ahead of her up the trail. She couldn't make out the words, but she thought she could distinguish two different voices.

Rosie reached for her two-way. One of the voices could be Colby. She felt her heart beat faster. He might be right ahead of her. If one of the voices was Colby's, then he would be close enough to receive her two-way call.

But the two-way wasn't there. Frantically, she searched her pockets, looked in her backpack. Then she remembered. She had taken it off her belt to get to the baton, back where the dead man lay. She left it in the snow. She cursed. Now she couldn't contact Colby and had no way to reach Dave once he arrived at Wilson's Folly. Moreover, Dave couldn't contact her either. What would he think when she didn't answer his call?

She had never felt so alone in her life. She wanted to scream in frustration and she longed to sit down and cry. She wanted so much to see Dave appear on the trail in front of her. But she struggled her backpack on and started out again.

"No time for regrets, woman," Rosie mumbled to herself. "You've got work to do and people to find."

A few yards up, she left the trail, walking backward, scuffing out her footprints as she went. She hoped anyone who might be trouble would mistake the indented snow as an animal's track traveling across the trail into the woods. But Dave would understand. She left one of her gloves, her initials printed inside, stuck on a branch, pointing the way she was going.

As she merged into the thicker woods, she turned around, bent low and moved toward the sound of the voices. She was getting closer. Then the voices disappeared.

The wind whipping the branches up into a flurry of creaking and crashing might have blocked the sound. Perhaps the two people had moved on up the trail out of hearing. The only voices she heard now were the frantic cawing of crows.

Rosie kept on. At last, the wind died down and the crows quieted. She picked up the sound of human talking again, closer than before. She bent lower and moved more slowly. She ducked from tree to tree, hoping she wouldn't be spotted. She still couldn't make out what was being said, but she could tell the voices came from two men.

She crept closer. Evidently, the men were not moving because their voices grew more distinct. She could catch some of the words now. Although she held her breath and strained to hear, she couldn't make sense of what they were saying. She heard their voices grow louder and guessed they were arguing.

Rosie dropped to her hands and knees and crawled through the deep snow, trying to keep her face above the white surface. When she could hear the voices enough to recognize the words, she stopped behind a tree. She drew up into a squat and peered out.

Two men were standing up to their knees in snow in a small clearing. Face to face, clouds of steam puffing from their mouths, they yelled at each other. They were dressed head to toe in hunter's garb and each carried a rifle.

"I don't get it. What're we doing here? We should leave while we have the chance."

"I told you, I'm not going back until I find it. If we go back and don't have the money, he'll probably shoot us all. And if you hadn't shot Beson, we'd have it now."

"You know I had to shoot him. He was going to shoot us. It was him or us. What'd you want me to do? Let him kill us?"

"No. But couldn't you have shot him in the arm or shoulder? We needed him to show us where it is. Now we only have Sully's directions to follow."

"His directions got us nothing but trouble. Let's just

call it quits and get off this mountain before we're snowed in."

"I told you. I'm not leaving until I find it. And if you do, I'll tell the boss you took the money and ran. He'll hunt you down, pluck out your eyes and stick them where the sun never shines. Wise up. It can't be too much farther to the hut. Sully said Beson told him it was under some rock up near the hut."

"You go on, then, Little Boss. Tell Big Boss whatever you want. I'm going back. This whole trip's too freaking dangerous. Who knows what Beson's spilled? We should have killed him during the robbery. We should have just left things as we planned. We should never have come back here. Now Beson's body's out there. Someone's gonna find it and then they'll be on to us. Be smart. We can come back another time. The money's safe where it is."

The short man turned away and started walking toward the trail. The tall man put his rifle on his shoulder and took aim at the retreating man's back.

Rosie decided she needed to intervene before someone else died. She'd heard enough to be certain they were responsible for the dead man she had found. The one they called Beson.

She removed her gun from her holster and stood up.

She took a couple of steps closer and was just about to ease out from behind her cover when a hand covered her mouth and another hand grabbed her gun. The hands forced her face down in the snow. She felt knees on her back making it impossible for her to move. A voice whispered, "Don't make a sound. Just listen."

THIRTY-TWO

ELLIE WOKE UP, STARTLED by Buddy's barking and the sound of the front door opening. At first, she was confused and thought she was lying in the woods and the murderer found her. However, when Margaret bent over her, she remembered the fall she took and the agonizing walk back to her house.

"Ellie, you look terrible. But don't you worry. We've come to take you down to the doctor. Look at her, Bonnie. She's pale as a ghost."

"Now don't go scaring her," Millie Buckley said. "Ellie, how do you feel?"

Ellie looked at her three friends. Bundled up in down parkas, Millie and Bonnie were dripping melting snow with each step. On the other hand, Margaret wore a stunning teal cashmere coat and scarf, which seemed to hold the snowflakes like little diamonds. All wore expressions of concern.

"I have a rather bad headache. Otherwise, I think I'm okay. A little confused, maybe."

"We're dying to know what happened to you, dear. Tell us everything, with all the dirty details," Margaret said as she sat down next to Ellie.

"Margaret, don't you think conversation can wait until later? First things first. Let's get her to the doctor," said Bonnie.

"I suppose you're right. But promise you'll tell us about your adventure before you tell anyone else. Will you? And don't worry about a thing. We're here to take care of you. Bonnie, you put her coat and hat on her and I'll tackle her boots," said Margaret, taking charge, as she loved to do.

Owning the most successful art gallery in Hummingbird Falls gave her some power and she used it whenever she could. She swept her bright teal cashmere scarf aside, removed her Italian leather gloves and placed them carefully on the end table. Then she bent down and started to fit Ellie's still-wet boots on her feet.

"Ow. My foot doesn't bend backward, Margaret. Take it easy."

Millie stepped in. "I'll put her boots on, Margaret. After all, I've put boots on three kids for many years and you've only had to put your own on. There's a trick to it."

Millie knelt down and gently pushed Ellie's foot into the boot. "Am I doing it right?"

Ellie nodded. "Yes, perfect. Thanks, Millie. I'm not used to someone getting me dressed."

The three women bustled around, putting more wood on the fire, making sure the kitchen stove was off, and filling Buddy's food and water dishes.

"Oh, no, if Buddy doesn't go, I'm not going either. I'm not leaving him here alone in this storm. Who knows when I'll get back."

Faced with another challenge the three friends looked at each other.

Margaret said, "Look, Ellie. I'm going to make an exception this one time and only because it's you. My new Saab has never had an animal in it and I swore it never would. But this one time, just this one time, I'll permit Buddy to ride in the backseat. He'll have to sit on a blanket, though."

Ellie smiled. "Thank you. Thanks so much for coming up here for me and for letting Buddy come with us, too. I have to admit I'm in no state to be driving myself. My head still hurts so much. I guess the pain's a sure sign I should see a doctor, just to be sure. So, thank you for caring for me. You're good friends. The kind I can count on to be there for me. It's turned out to be quite a fall. If I ever needed friends, I sure need them now."

All four women had tears in the corner of their eyes by the end of Ellie's short speech. Then Margaret swooped up her gloves and got on one side of Ellie while Bonnie got on the other side. They grabbed under her arms and helped her off the couch.

"Wait a minute. My head's spinning. Just wait until it stops, please."

After a few minutes, Ellie said, "Okay. It stopped. Let's go."

They walked slowly to the door. Snow rushed in on a gust of wind as Millie opened the door and waited for Margaret and Bonnie to steer Ellie outside.

The women and Buddy trudged carefully through the snow-filled front walk to Margaret's red Saab, parked in the driveway. Margaret clicked her remote, the car lights turned on and the doors unlocked.

"You sit in back with Millie and Buddy, Ellie. I think it'll be more comfortable for you. Bonnie, you sit up here with me." Margaret was directing again.

"Where're we going?" Ellie asked.

"To Doc Muller's office. He's closest," Bonnie said. "Okay with you?"

Bonnie's talent for compassion was a sharp contrast

to Margaret's need to control. Hummingbird Falls's residents knew Bonnie was always patient, engaging and caring in her job as a clerk at the town hall.

"Fine. I'm just going to close my eyes until we get there."

"Here," Millie said. "Put your head on my shoulder and go to sleep if you want. I'll hold you steady."

Ellie was grateful Millie was the touchy-feely motherly type. Right now, close physical contact was more soothing than all the words in the world. She snuggled her head onto Millie's shoulder, closed her eyes, and held on to Buddy as the Saab slowly moved down the long driveway and soon disappeared into the whiteout of snow.

THIRTY-THREE

EVERYTHING HAPPENED at once. The snow-loaded hemlock branches had absorbed enough warmth from the hunter's fire to start the snow melting. The three hunters ignored the dripping, intent on cooking their meal. They hadn't read the page in Jim's survivor book warning about the danger of building a fire under a tree laden with snow. Now the snow was starting to slip like an avalanche, preparing to bury them and their fire.

Old Scar Face stood like a statue just outside the bent-down branches of the hemlock tree, gathering his strength and courage. He was waiting for the right time to hurdle through the drooping limbs to the food he could smell, just out of his reach.

He didn't have to wait long. Great heaps of thumping snow hit the ground in loud clumps. The tree limbs dumped their snow. Then they sprang upward, freed of their weight.

Scar Face saw men sprawled under piles of snow, a chaos of food, clothes, wood, scattered everywhere. The fire was gone, buried under the snow. He sprang through the long hemlock branches toward the food he was hunting. His focus was limited. The instinct to survive drove him to ignore his most feared enemy, the men. He stepped on them as if they were logs in his way.

When he felt resistance, he swept his huge paw at them, clawing them away from the food he was claiming. His nose hunted for the morsels of food that might keep him alive another winter.

The mounds of snow descending and the whipping up of the bare branches shocked the three hunters. They sat, helpless, as the snow dumped on them. Snow buried their fire and plunged their shelter into darkness.

Before they could figure out what had happened and what to do, something huge crashed into them. They wallowed in the dark, fighting piles of snow, tossed-around equipment and a massive creature. They struggled to free themselves and escape the monster that had appeared out of nowhere.

Screams rose into the cold air. The hunters fought to free themselves, but the weight of the snow slowed them down. Disoriented in the darkness and without flashlights or firelight, they were confused and terrified. The huge beast thrashed around them; his massive body filled the small shelter. Old Scar Face was causing havoc as he slammed around hunting for the food the hunters had cooked.

They knew they should find their rifles, but they wanted to get away from the awful creature more. They were terrified. On hands and knees, they crawled as fast as they could away from the bear, out of the shelter, toward the open. Old Scar Face was so intent on finding and eating the buried food, he paid no attention to the fleeing hunters, glad they were out of his way.

Once outside the shelter of the tree, Bob ran in one direction, Andy and Jim in another. While they were running Andy and Jim grabbed for their sidearms, but only Bob had his Glock. The others had put their equipment belts with their guns next to the tree trunk with their day packs and rifles. Bob had kept his equipment belt on, his Glock holstered.

When the three men realized the bear was not pursuing them, they gathered behind a tree.

"I don't have my gun," Andy whispered.

"I don't have a gun, either," Jim said. "What'll we do? Let's run for it."

Bob turned around and held up his hand. "I've got my Glock. You two, stay behind me, now."

He pointed the gun in his shaking hand at the hemlock tree as his two friends moved behind him. They were moving backward, away from the bear as fast as they could in the deep snow. As they reached the edge of the clearing, Bob noticed snow was accumulating on Andy and Jim's shoulders and heads. They didn't have their coats or hats.

"Damn it. You haven't even got your parkas. Stop."

As the three men stared at each other, Bob said, "We can't run. You won't survive in this cold for an hour without your coats. We're going to have to hide and wait until he goes so we can get our gear. Or we're going to have to kill him." Bob groaned. "Otherwise, we won't make it."

Old Scar Face rutted around under the tree. The men could hear him clawing through the snow, looking for their food. He had paid no attention when the screaming men fled. He sensed they were out in the clearing, but his need to fill his stomach overcame his caution. He gorged on the hot dogs, bacon, cheese, stew-flavored snow and trail mix. He scraped at the piles of snow, uncovering morsels, piece by piece. He pawed at the cold coals of the fire and ate the partially cooked potatoes. He was looking around for more when the bullet hit him.

Old Scar Face roared with pain, turned to look at the hot spot burning into his thick back. He stood on his back legs and pawed the air. Then he dropped to all fours, charged out from under the tree and ran for the safety of the woods.

Unfortunately, the three men foolishly took their stand several yards in front of the opening under the tree, to get a better shot at the bear. But, they were also blocking the bear's escape. Standing between Scar Face and liberty, they were unavoidable targets.

Old Scar Face had no choice. Frenzied by the painful agony in his back and trapped by the enemy in front of him, he charged right into the men. Shots rang out. With teeth bared and paws swatting, he fought to make a path through them to freedom. Screams rose again, as a cuff of Old Scar Face's paw or a bite from his long teeth caught the surprised hunters. Two of them fell and the other backed off, leaving Old Scar Face his chance. The bear ran into the woods and disappeared.

THIRTY-FOUR

DOC MULLER'S OFFICE was dark and the door locked. A note fastened to the bulletin board out front stated the doctor was on an emergency call and would not be back today. He referred patients to the emergency room at the Greenberg Memorial Hospital or the walk-in clinic just south of Hummingbird Falls. Margaret chose the walk-in clinic.

The four women and Buddy trooped into the clinic and stopped at the receptionist's desk. When Margaret explained the situation, the receptionist took Ellie by the arm, who took Buddy by the leash, and led them to a small cubicle. She helped Ellie climb up on the examining table, then took her temperature and blood pressure, gently cleaned the wound on her forehead and took a brief health history.

Ellie didn't have to wait too long. The nurse practitioner introduced herself as Carmen Gomez. She patted Buddy as she scanned Ellie's health history and asked Ellie to explain what she was feeling and where.

She flipped on a strong light and directed it at the wound on Ellie's forehead. Then did the same with the bump on the back of her head. Carmen carefully felt the bump as Ellie winced. She asked Ellie some more questions and then directed Ellie to lie on her stomach. Carmen talked quietly to Ellie, explaining what she was doing as she focused the light on the bump and closely examined the swollen area on the back of Ellie's head. She picked up a pair of tweezers.

"I don't think this will hurt, but I'm going to pick out a splinter from your scalp."

Carmen gave a little tug with the tweezers. "Got it."

"Ouch," Ellie gasped.

Buddy jumped up barking.

"I'm okay, Buddy. Lie down."

Buddy looked at Ellie and then lay back down.

Carmen continued. "There was some foreign material adhered to skin around the contusion on your head. You said you had a wool hat on, didn't you? Do you have the hat with you?"

Ellie pointed to the chair where she had dumped her coat and hat. Carmen examined the hat under the light, turning it slowly until she found what she was looking for. She used the tweezers again and then handled the hat back to Ellie. She held out the tweezers for Ellie to see.

"Looks like a twig."

"It is a twig. It was stuck in your hat. This is what I found at the base of the bump on your head."

Carmen held out a small piece of bark. "It looks like your attacker was a maple tree."

"What?" Ellie asked. "What do you mean?"

"My guess is when you were pushing back tree limbs, a maple branch snapped back at you pretty hard. It hit you with enough power to throw you off balance. Then your head hit the rock."

"You mean my attacker was just a branch?"

"I'm pretty sure of it. If a human smacked you with a branch, or a stick, the injury would be worse, at a different angle and most likely would have cut through the scalp. There would have been a lot of bleeding. You have a good-size bump, but it's not bleeding. When the branch hit you, the slam was strong enough to throw you forward. You lost your balance. The hit of your temple against the rock was what caused you to pass out."

"Well, I'll be. It sure hurts. I thought someone hit me."

"Oh, I'm sure it hurts a lot. The bump may hurt, but fortunately it's not serious. The cut on your forehead's not a concern, either. You don't even need stitches."

"Then I'm okay?"

"Well, I didn't say you're okay, exactly. The cut will heal in a few days and the bump will go down. However, you might have a slight concussion from hitting the rock so hard. You need to rest and stay still for at least twenty-four hours. If your head's still painful then we'll probably have to do a head scan. If the pain decreases over the next few hours and your nausea passes, then you should be fine."

"I feel better already, just hearing what you said. When I was so dizzy and confused, when I couldn't remember who that familiar face was, I was worried maybe I had a serious injury."

Carmen smiled at Ellie. "Not too serious, thank goodness."

"Well, lately I haven't been able to remember things like I used to. In the Greenberg robbery, I saw something that I still can't remember. Then this morning, I couldn't remember again. I thought I might be getting senile. I was afraid I was losing my memory. I couldn't live with that."

Carmen gave Ellie a strange look.

"I thought about my mother when she got older and started to forget things. I felt so sorry for her. She was diagnosed with Alzheimer's. For the last several months and for a moment out there in the woods, I was afraid I had it, too. I know you don't just come down with Alzheimer's, but back when I gained consciousness, my thoughts were very dark."

"Understandable. You had a bad fall. You were just confused and probably scared."

"You don't see any signs of Alzheimer's or senility, do you? I worry because I love to paint and write poetry, solve mysteries, read and see the birds and the wilderness and…I'm running on now, aren't I?"

"What did you say about solving mysteries?"

"I just keep running into, or rather the mysteries just keep running into me. Believe me, I don't look for them. Like today. Buddy led me to the dead body. I wasn't looking for it. No way would I look for a dead body, but dead bodies seem to be placed in my way lately."

"And these are the mysteries you're talking about?"

"You do think I'm crazy, don't you?"

"No. I'd just like to hear more about the mysteries you run into."

"There are a lot. Like who broke all my bird feeders, what happened to Josie, who killed Alice, who sent all those riddles to me, why the Buckleys came to town, how intelligent the crows are, how did that man in the woods die, why the hummingbirds fight so much…"

"Ellie, stop. That's okay. I get it, I think. You're a woman who's curious, loves to figure out things and find out what she doesn't know. You're certainly not crazy or senile as far as I can see. Or if you are, then I am, too. Why do you think I became a nurse practitioner? For the same reasons. To figure out what's going on with my patients. We have a lot in common. I'd never call myself or anyone else crazy for wanting to learn more. I'd call them smart and inquisitive. An investigator type."

Ellie sat still for a moment. "You do understand, don't you? Thanks for not doubting my sanity. Sometimes, well, often, my mouth gets ahead of my thoughts and then I know I sound stupid, appear frazzled, or befuddled. I'm working on it, trying to change, think before I talk."

Carmen nodded, listening. Her black eyes matched the color of her curly short hair. She smiled as Ellie talked, her tiny wrinkles framing her lovely eyes.

"Good for you. Well, I'm glad to meet you, Ellie, and all the many aspects of you."

"I'm glad to meet you, too. You know, I thought at first the murderer might still be in the woods. I was afraid he'd kill me so I couldn't tell where the body was. I'd much rather be attacked by a maple. So, I thank you. This time you solved the mystery and so quickly. I'm relieved my attacker was just a maple tree. You figured it all out by looking at the clues, not by just imagining."

"Well you weren't so confused you didn't recognize the killer could still be out there. Did you contact the police?"

"Oh, yes. Howie, the fire chief, is going out after the body with some volunteers. I understand Dave, Rosie and Colby are up at the notch looking into something up there. Have you heard about it?"

"Ellie, you've done all you can. My advice is to forget about what Dave and Howie are doing and instead focus on yourself and your health. Fortunately, you don't have any symptoms other than the headache, vertigo and nausea. If those pass, then you don't have a concussion. Let everything else go for now. Rest. Eat. Talk with your friends. Call me tomorrow and let me know how you feel."

"Okay. Thanks, Carmen. I hope to see you again, only under different circumstances."

"Me, too. I'll probably see you at the Pastry Shop sometime. Now try to eat something and see if you can hold it down and don't forget to call me if you feel worse. I'll be waiting for your call tomorrow morning about how you're doing."

Ellie hugged Carmen goodbye. Ellie and Buddy walked unaided to the waiting room and told the good news to their friends. She paid her bill and then turned to the group.

"Let's go to the Pastry Shop, my treat. Carmen said I should try to eat something. And I haven't eaten anything but a dog biscuit for hours."

"A dog biscuit?" the three women chorused together.

"One of Henry's. They're not bad with honey on them."

"Are you sure you're okay? Maybe you should be resting," Bonnie said.

"A dog biscuit?" Margaret asked, scowling. "Did you tell the doctor? Maybe you'll be poisoned, too."

"Stop it, you two. Those biscuits are good. My kids have snacked on them more than once and they're very much alive, trust me," Millie added with a smile.

"Thank you, Millie. I knew I wasn't the only one

who ever ate a dog biscuit. I'll rest after we visit the Pastry Shop. I promise."

The four women and Buddy piled into the Saab again and slowly made their way through the snowy streets to the Pastry Shop.

THIRTY-FIVE

HOWIE, HIS CREW OF volunteers and Doc Mueller had been trudging through the deep snow on the old Jefferson Trail for almost an hour when they saw a red scarf blowing in the snowy breeze.

"There it is," Howie cried. "Ellie's scarf. This's where we cut into the woods. Be careful. Keep your eyes open for anything unusual."

They moved single file, each trying to step into the footprints of the one who went before. The snow had filled in Ellie and Buddy's indentations made hours before and the snow lay untouched before them.

After a while, they spotted the other red scarf. They stopped and huddled in a circle.

Howie said, "Let's stop and look around from here. Does anyone see a mound where a body could be?"

Everyone stared through the falling snow.

Wendy said, "There's a hump over there, just before the big oak."

Paul interrupted. "I think I see a big mound behind the fallen log on the left. I bet the body's there."

He started to walk forward. Howie grabbed him by the arm.

"Hold on, Paul. We have to do this by the book."

"I'll be careful. I've read all the books. I know how they do it."

"Wait. Simon, do you see anything? Bill? Chen? Doc?"

The others shook their heads no. Doc Muller spoke up.

"From the shape and size, I'd guess Paul's right. I think the body has to be behind the log. The hump in front of the oak tree is too short."

The others studied the two bumps in the snow and nodded in agreement.

"All right. Doc, you walk over and check it out. We'll stay here so there isn't too much disturbance of the scene until you've determined the body's there."

Doc Muller walked to the log and looked down at the raised area. He squatted down and scooped snow off one end. He dug deeper. Then he stood up and called, "Yep, it's here."

"Can you tell who he is? Do you recognize him?"

"Nope. Never saw him before, to my knowledge. Maybe one of you can identify him."

"Hold on." Howie put his arm up to stop the group from moving closer to the body. "Can you look for a pulse or make sure he's dead?"

"No question he's dead," Doc answered. "He's blue, eyes glazed. But I'll check his pulse just to make you happy." He placed his hand on the man's throat, feeling for a pulse.

"Nothing. He's dead. Let me scoop off some more snow and see if I can find out what happened to him."

While Doc brushed snow off and examined the body, the others stamped their feet to keep them warm and talked in low voices.

"Who do you think it is? I hope I don't recognize him. He could've been here for months, I suppose. Has anyone turned up missing lately?" All questions and no answers.

Doc stood up again. "Well, he's got no coat on, just an orange vest. And he's ripped wide open. Rodents been at him. But I don't think he died here. I'm pretty sure he didn't actually die at all."

"What? What are you saying?" The volunteers strained forward.

"Howie, I think it's safe for everyone to come on over here now. I don't imagine we'll hurt this crime scene any."

Howie hesitated. "You sure, Doc?"

"Positive. Come see for yourselves."

Paul led the pack. They crowded around the body. They gaped. They shifted their feet and then one by one they began to laugh. First Doc, then Wendy, followed by Simon, Chen and Bill. Only Paul failed to laugh and looked from the body to the others' faces. He looked a little green.

"What's going on?"

They just laughed harder. Tears rolled down Wendy's cheeks, mixing with the snowflakes melted from the flush on her face.

"Paul, did you go to the Ghoulog?"

"The what?"

"The Ghoulog. You know, the big haunting event on the top of Canton Mountain. They have it every year in October," said Bill.

Wendy chimed in, "It was terrific this year. Very creepy and lots of scary scenes. Like a haunted house, only the haunts were outside as well as inside and done up beyond what you could ever imagine."

Chen said, "The Ghoulog's so frightening and gross no one under ten is allowed to attend."

"Gross, like ripped open bodies and heads spitting

blood and hanging people who're still wiggling. Things follow you in the dark and jump out at you. You can't use a flashlight either," Simon said. "I loved it."

"I don't like things like scary houses," said Paul. "I'd never go to one of those things. It sounds sick. Anyway, what does the Ghoulog have to do with this guy?"

Doc Muller said, "Paul, bend down and look at the body. Touch his face. Look at the chest wound."

"Why? I don't want to get near it. I really don't need to look closely. Besides, it smells. Even in this cold air, you can still smell it. Worse than any plumbing disaster I've ever had to deal with and I can tell you about a few of those. Why, just last week…"

"Okay, Paul. We don't need to hear about it," Wendy chimed in.

"Too much information," Bill added.

"I thought you liked things like this, Paul. You told us you read a lot of mystery books, about forensics and police procedure," Howie said.

"Reading's different from seeing the real thing. I don't have to see or touch dead things when I read. You can't make me touch a dead body."

"No," said Doc. "But this body isn't dead."

"What?" stammered Paul. "It's still alive?"

"Nope," answered Doc as the others laughed. "It wasn't ever alive."

"You mean it's like a vampire or a zombie? Kind of not alive? Forget it. You're just teasing me. Of course, it was alive. And now, of course, it's dead."

"Check it out, Paul. It isn't dead or alive and never was."

Paul looked from one face to the other and then

down at the body. He grimaced at the blue face, the glazed eyes, and the intestines half in and half out of the wound.

"Then what is it?" he whispered.

THIRTY-SIX

"IT'S A GHOULOG BODY! A dummy from the haunting. It's not real," Doc declared.

"I don't believe it. What's the smell, then? Something died," said Paul.

Chen answered. "Looks like lots of rotten chicken and deer guts to me. I think this cadaver was the patient in the surgery where the surgeon brother scooped out all the body organs. It was a ghastly scene."

Paul took a step closer. Holding his nose, he looked down at the body. He started to gag. "Wow, it sure looks real. You're certain, Doc?"

"Positive. Obviously, one of the Ghoulog boys dumped it here. Why? I don't know. We'll have to ask them, I guess."

"What'll we do with it, Doc?" asked Chen.

"Let's pack it in a body bag and bring it back to show Dave. He may want to check it out. Besides, we don't want any other innocent hikers to freak out thinking they've found a dead man."

Laughing with relief because they had recovered a dummy and not a real corpse, the group folded it up and pushed it into a body bag. Wendy and Chen each grabbed a side to carry it down the trail.

"Your turn next, Paul," Wendy cried out.

"I don't think so. I'm not getting near it. I still can't

believe anyone could create something so disgusting and think it's fun. What were they thinking of? The whole idea's so gross. And you people paid to see it? It's hard to imagine. Ugh."

Shaking his head, Paul followed the others down the trail, staying as far away from the Ghoulog corpse as he could.

THIRTY-SEVEN

DAVE, JAMES, MIKE, Reggie and the three search dogs arrived at Wilson's Folly parking lot. The two Hummingbird Falls police SUVs and one large black four-wheel-drive truck were the only vehicles in the lot and they were mounded with snow.

"Over there, Mike. Park so you block the exit. I don't want anyone coming or going before we check them out," Dave directed.

Mike positioned his truck across the access road to the parking lot.

The four men walked over to the SUVs and the truck.

"You guys check the SUVs. I'll check out the truck," Dave ordered.

He walked over to the truck, slipped under the crime tape and scraped snow off the back window. He peered in. His breath fogged up the window and he wiped it off again. He walked around to the other side of the truck and repeated his actions. He shook his head and joined the others at the SUVs.

"See anything out of line?" he asked.

"Nope. Both vehicles look perfectly ordinary as far as I can see," Mike said. "What about the truck?"

"Rosie was right. Blood's all over the backseat. Looks like there was a struggle and someone lost quite a bit of blood. If there's a blood trail, leading from the truck, it's buried under all this snow by now."

"The dogs can pick it up. The snow shouldn't bother them too much," Mike said.

"Okay. Try the dogs. See what they can do. We'll start near the truck and then move up trail where Rosie told me she was going. Hopefully she's connected with Colby by now."

While Dave tried to reach Rosie and Colby by cell phone, Mike headed back to his truck and released his dogs from their carriers, leashed them and brought them over to the New Jersey truck. He gave the signal to start work. Noses pushed deep into the snow, the dogs snuffed around the truck several times, and then one started baying and pulling Mike away from the lot and toward the trailhead.

Dave gave up on the cell and was trying the two-way. No one responded. He turned back to Mike and Reggie.

"Nobody's answering the two-ways. I don't understand it. I know Rosie had hers. She couldn't reach Colby by cell and by two-way. Whether he couldn't answer or didn't receive the message isn't clear. Rosie talked with Stan at the Wilson's hut on the two-way so her two-way was working. But now, I can't get Rosie, Colby or Stan to answer. Something strange's going on."

"That's weird," Reggie answered. "Maybe the storm's blocking the signal. I've used a two-way up here and it always worked for me."

"Could be the storm, but whatever it is, I don't like it. What's up with the dogs, Mike?"

"They've picked up on something. Could be Rosie, since she was the last one here," Mike called.

"Someone has to stay in the parking lot to stop people from coming in or leaving. The rest of us will follow the dogs," Dave said. "I guess we'd better hold everyone trying to leave until we know what's going on. If they make a fuss, tell them to take it up with me when I get back. Who wants to stay here?"

The men looked at each other. James answered. "I guess it better be me. I haven't hiked in snow for a long time and I'm not in very good shape. But I do know how to reason with people and calm them down. Soothing troubled folks was part of my training as a counselor. I can try to keep them quiet if they end up having to wait before they can leave."

"Okay. James, you stay. Mike, Reggie, you come with me."

Reggie said, "I packed sandwiches, bottled water and hot coffee in thermoses for each of us. Some cookies, too. Fresh from the deli."

"Thanks, Reggie," Dave said. "Smart idea. We'll need to keep hydrated and energized. It's not going to be easy to climb up this steep a trail in the snow. Rosie said it's icy higher up."

"Let's get going before it gets worse," said Mike, holding the straining dogs.

The men secured their backpacks, put on snowshoes and headed toward the trailhead. Snow blasted into them, quickly coating their hoods and the fronts of their parkas. Clouds of steamy breath rose from the group as they picked up speed.

James lost sight of them when they reached the trees. He walked to Mike's truck, jumped in and sat back, drinking the coffee Reggie left and scanning the white world around him. The truck was running and heat flowed from the heater. James removed his gloves and unzipped his parka. He wished he were going with them, but knew he would have slowed them down. He was nervous, being alone, and hoped nobody gave him any trouble. Dave had quietly slipped him a gun, saying "Just in case," but James wasn't about to shoot anyone. At least he hoped he wouldn't have to.

The trail was snowed in. No sign of anyone coming or going. Mike kept the dogs on leash because of the poor visibility.

The men and dogs trudged along at a good pace for a while. Then the footing became more difficult. The snow lay deeper the higher they climbed and they struggled to break through the heavy drifts.

They took turns handling the dogs and breaking trail as the lead man grew exhausted quickly. In some places, the wind pushed the snow into giant drifts, some three to five feet in depth. If they couldn't go around the drift, the first man would wade into it, shoving snow with hands and legs, working up a sweat. The men following pushed through easier, but still exerted much energy.

Other places, the wind blew the ground bare. Snowshoes hindered rather than helped in these sections. Dogs and men slipped on the icy frozen ground. Trying to make headway on this terrain was nearly impossible. The men took their snowshoes off and carried them, and put on ice cleats until they hit deeper snow. Then they had to stop and do the reverse. It was slow going.

Dave stopped frequently to try the cell phone and the two-way. It was like spitting in the wind. His calls went out and whipped back in his face. No response from Stan, Rosie or Colby.

The group eventually reached the birch-tree blow-down. They stopped and stared. The snow-covered stumps, like wooden headstones, reminded them of all the lost trees.

"Look. Over there," Reggie yelled as he pointed to a stick rising above the snow. Tied to it, a piece of yellow crime-scene tape thrashed back and forth with the wind.

They moved toward it. Crows rose into the air, startling them. They cawed a warning, then wheeled off into the snowy sky and disappeared. The men continued plowing toward the marker.

"Damn crows. Scared me," Reggie said.

Mike answered, "You know, they're awfully smart, those crows. I've seen it happen again and again. They figure something out before a human can. Maybe because they can fly over and see what's around. But it's spooky. It's almost as if they were watching the stick, waiting for us, making sure we found it."

"Well, they flew up trail. Maybe they will show us where Rosie and Colby are," Reggie said.

"I wouldn't be surprised," Mile responded. "I've heard stories of them leading lost folks out of the woods."

"Careful," Dave intervened, "don't come too close until I see what's up. Rosie must have marked this spot for a reason, or maybe Colby did. Let me check it out."

Dave took the lead and slowly made his way to the marker.

"Snow's been pushed around. Whatever's under here is blanketed again." Dave paused to catch his breath. "Could be Rosie or Colby found something and marked the spot. Not too long ago. Only about another five inches has piled up since."

Dave brushed some of the new snow away carefully. "Well, just what I was afraid of. It's a body. Half his head's blown away. Could be a hunter, guessing from the orange vest."

He continued to brush the snow away, uncovering the body. He checked for a pulse, even though it was obvious the man was dead. He looked for the cause of death, careful not to move the body.

"Shot. In the face. The splatter and tissue in the snow around his head indicates someone shot him here. There's a stab wound in his shoulder. Looks like another stab wound in the right leg. Not much blood in the snow around the stab wounds. Maybe the blood in the truck is his. Now, the gunshot could result from a hunting accident, but I've never heard of a hunter dying from a stabbing accident. Somehow, I don't believe he was hunting. His clothes seem more suitable for hiking than hunting, other than the vest, which is a safety matter. No sign of a gun or rifle or any other equipment that I can see. Could be buried, I suppose."

Reggie and Mike looked at the body silently. Mike said, "Lonely way to die. Stabbed, then shot halfway up a mountain and left buried in the snow."

Dave was searching the man's pockets. "No ID. No wallet. No hunting license. With his face blown away, it might be hard to get identification."

"If it were a hunting accident, wouldn't someone have called it in?" Mike asked.

"That's my thinking, too," Dave said. "We didn't get any calls about a hunter being shot. Colby's message said something about a hunter, maybe lost, but not dead.

Maybe he hadn't found him yet. He mentioned a gun, I'm pretty sure. No gun here, though, unless it's buried under the snow somewhere. Maybe Colby took it. No sense digging through the snow to try to find anything. It'd be a waste of time, most likely."

"I guess we can assume Rosie came along later and found him," Reggie said. "She marked it with the tape, but kept going on up. I wonder if she saw someone or something. Maybe she could see footprints when she was here. For some reason she kept on."

"Rosie would keep going until she found Colby. I think she stumbled across the body and marked it, so we could find it later. But I don't think she saw Colby, so she continued to look for him. We'd better do the same."

The men drank some hot coffee, ate part of their sandwiches and fed the dogs some beef jerky, and then plowed on. Frequently, they would call out Rosie or Colby's name or try the two-way, but received no response.

As the afternoon moved toward dusk, the snow started to let up. The searchers were able to see farther ahead and make better time as the wind tapered off and the dark storm clouds began to hustle east. Dave and the others scanned the landscape for other markers or mounds, but found nothing.

"Wouldn't Rosie or Colby leave us a sign they'd been here?" Mike asked. His dogs were still eager to push on. They'd plunge their noses deep into the snow, pull them out, run a few steps and thrust their noses in again.

"Not necessarily," Dave answered, although he was wondering the same thing. Why hadn't his officers left something behind, signaling their whereabouts?

"Maybe the wind took it," Dave said. What he didn't say was, maybe they were prisoners, or worse, dead.

"At least we can see up the trail. Doesn't look like there're any obstructions ahead."

Dave didn't respond. The fact the trail looked smooth with no obvious mounds was a good thing. Another mound could mean another dead body, and this time it might be Colby's or Rosie's. But seeing no sign, no footsteps, no markers wasn't good. Where were his two officers? What had happened to them? A feeling of dread stole over him, like the black storm cloud that sneaked over the mountains this morning, heralding dangerous times ahead.

THIRTY-EIGHT

ELLIE SAT DOWN in a booth and Buddy lay down next to the table, while Millie, Margaret and Bonnie went to pick up their orders. Several other village residents were waiting out the storm in the warm and sweet-smelling Pastry Shop.

Bobby, the youngest worker on the road crew, was taking a well-earned break from shoveling the village's sidewalks and fire hydrants. When he noticed Ellie wearing a bandage on her forehead, he called out to her.

"Hey, Mrs. Hastings. You okay? Looks like a serious bandage."

"I'm fine, Bobby, but thanks for asking. Turns out I got attacked by a maple tree."

Ellie went on to explain how the maple tree attacked her. Listeners laughed at her tale. She didn't bother to mention she might have a concussion and how her head was aching. She left out the part about the dead body, too, not wanting to cause a scene before Dave informed any relatives of the man's death or released his identity to the public.

Bonnie carried Ellie's hazelnut coffee and two blueberry turnovers to the booth.

"Oh, two. No, I can't. I started my…well, I'm trying to…I really shouldn't, you know."

"Now Ellie, be quiet and eat. You need to keep your

strength up. Carmen said we needed to see you eat without feeling nauseous. So just nibble a little on one, for me, will you?"

"Well, if it's absolutely necessary," Ellie replied as she picked up her fork and cut a big piece of turnover and stuffed it in her mouth. "Umm. This tastes really good."

Buddy looked up at her and licked his chops. Ellie leaned over and patted him. She whispered, "Just this once. Back on the diet tomorrow."

Buddy whined in reply.

The other women carried their coffee and pastries over and sat down. "You're starting to look a little better, Ellie," said Margaret. "You've got some color back. How's your head feel?"

"Much better, thanks to you all. I think the caffeine in the coffee's helping," she answered as she finished the first turnover and looked at the second one.

"You ladies know about the big to-dos going on?" Bobby asked from his booth down back.

"No," said Bonnie. "I probably would've known if I was working at the town hall as usual, but we went up to rescue Ellie. What'd I miss?"

"I know you're usually the first to know, Bonnie, but this came straight from Larry. Dave, Reggie, Mike and James left earlier to go up to Wilson's Folly."

Several people asked, "Why? What's going on?"

Bobby puffed up as he realized everyone's attention focused on him. As the youngest member of the road crew, the designated gofer, he didn't often get a chance to shine. Even today with all the snow, he didn't get to run one of the snow plows. He was designated shoveler for the village. He was enjoying his extended break and eager to be the one who could relay the latest news.

"Seems Rosie was looking for Colby, who was ticketing vehicles up in the notch. He's missing up there."

A buzz of excited voices interrupted him. Bobby waited for the voices to quiet down and continued.

"Yep, they couldn't contact Colby, so Rosie drove up to find him." Bobby took a slow drink of his coffee.

The crowd hooted at him and called out, "Go on. Don't stop there, Bobby. What happened? Did Rosie find Colby?"

"All right, hold your horses. No, she couldn't find him, so Dave and them went up to look, too."

Another loud hum of voices swelled as everyone started talking at once. Questions and theories about what might be going on were on every lip.

The three women turned to Ellie. "You better hurry up and get over your head problem. There's a mystery needs solving."

"I'm sure Dave and the others have everything under control," Ellie said. "Although, it's interesting to ponder what happened to Colby, why Rosie couldn't find him and why Dave's so worried. But we'll probably find out very soon."

"Look, the storm's letting up," said Elizabeth, owner of the Pastry Shop. She was standing next to the big front window.

Everyone turned to look out the window. The wind had diminished to a breeze, lazily floating huge snowflakes here and there.

"That's a sure sign it's almost over, when the flakes get so big," said Elizabeth.

"And the sky's getting brighter, too," added Margaret. "This snow is going to bring the tourists. Yahoo! They'll snowshoe, ski, eat and, thank the heavens, shop. I'd better get on over to the gallery and open up. Can you gals get home without me?"

"My car's up at the Hawk's Inn. I'm due to work the dinner shift. I need a lift," said Millie.

"My car's right in the town-hall parking lot. I'll get it, drive you up there, Millie, and then drop Ellie and Buddy over to Sarah's. She said Ellie should stay in town tonight, just to be sure. That's why we packed her overnight bag."

"You did? I don't remember that," Ellie said. "I don't want to be a bother and it's much easier for you to drop me down here instead of driving all the way up the mountain road. Mike probably didn't have time to plow my driveway. So I'll take Sarah up on her offer. I'd like to be around when Dave returns, to see if there's anything I can help him with."

The others laughed. "You never change, even when you're bonked on the head, Ellie. When something's going on, you always want to be right in the center of it."

"Now, how can you say such a thing? That's not true. Things always happen when I'm around. They come to me. I don't go looking for mysteries to solve. I had nothing to do with Colby going missing. What would I know about it?"

"Well, somehow you're always at the right place at the right time," Bonnie said.

"Or is it the wrong place at the wrong time?" Margaret quipped.

"Oh, give me a break. This morning I went for a walk. How'd I know there was a dead body in the woods? How could I know Buddy would find it?"

The Pastry Shop roared with questions.

"What dead body? Who? Where? What happened? Is that how your head got hurt? Did someone try to murder you, too? Is there a murderer loose around here? Tell us."

"Okay. Okay. Wait. If you'll be quiet a second, I'll tell you," Ellie tried to be heard above the noise. The crowd quieted.

"It was really nothing," she began.

"You can protest all you want, Ellie, but I bet you a blueberry turnover, you'll be on the phone to Dave as soon as he shows up," said Margaret as she wrapped her gorgeous scarf around her neck.

"Well, if I am, it's only to clear things up about my fall. Betsy probably will tell him someone knocked me out and I need to let him know a maple branch snapped back and cracked my head, not a murderer. And he may want my eyewitness report on the body, how it was situated, if there were any tracks, that sort of thing."

"Now, he'll have to stop the wild rumors you folks invent. Otherwise, the whole town will be up in arms, talking about a mad forest killer rampaging through our woods," Bonnie said.

"But what about the body? How did it die? There must be a murderer if there was a body," Bobby yelled.

"Maybe a bear killed him," Ellie said.

"A bear? Was it a bear? Oh, no. A rogue bear. Did you hear about the bear in Washington State? He killed a man," the voices cried.

"Wait. Wait. I didn't see a bear. I don't know if a bear did it. All I know is I saw a dead body. Oh, my, how did this get started? I didn't plan to say anything about the body."

"Is the body still out there?" Bobby asked.

"I'm not sure. Howie and some volunteers went to get it, I think. Betsy might know more about it," Ellie replied. "She told me she was calling Howie because Dave, Rosie and Colby were on a case up at the notch. I didn't know Colby was missing, though."

"I saw the ambulance drive out quite a while ago," Jack, the village barber, related.

Karen Stilson, who retired from Greenberg's shoe factory a few years ago, added, "I saw some cars parked at the fire station. Thought it was odd when no fire calls were made."

"Who'd you see?" Bobby asked.

"Doc's car was there. Wendy Hill's truck, Chen's old Subaru, Howie's, of course. Maybe one more. Can't exactly remember. Oh, yes, Paul's plumbing van."

"Wow, they've got the volunteer crew going after the body," Jack said.

"I wonder what they'll find," Bobby said. "Boy, there's a lot going on in this little place."

Most everyone nodded. "You can say that again," Margaret said as she headed toward the door. "Bye, ladies and gentlemen, let me know what you find out. Call me at the gallery if anything more happens." Margaret swept her scarf back and glided out the door.

Bonnie stood up. "I really should get going, too. Debbie's done double duty while I was gone. I'll bring her a bag of cookies for a reward. Do you want to wait here while I pick up the car or do you want to walk with me to the town hall?"

"The snow's almost stopped and it's not very far. It'll do me good to get some air. Let's walk," said Ellie, putting Buddy's leash on. "And I can stop by the post office to show Sarah I'm on the mend, so she won't worry."

"Oh, she'll worry anyway. You know her," said Millie. "She worries about everyone and everything in this village. But we'll pop in and at least she can see you're walking and talking. It'll make her feel better."

The women waved goodbye to Elizabeth and the other patrons who were chatting back and forth feverishly about murderers and killer bears. They walked out into the cool air. Clouds were speeding across the sky, followed by a bright blue wash and signs of the upcoming sunset. The first snowfall of the year was now history.

A plow thundered by and the driver, Larry, honked the horn at the women as he cleared the last of the snow from the other side of the street. High piles of snow bordered the road. A big heap of slush filled the middle of the road.

The sun finally emerged and even though it was close to dropping down behind the mountains, the temperature started to climb a little. Cars began to appear, some stopping at the Pastry Shop, some at the post office, others headed across the covered bridge on their way down to Greenberg and the ski slopes. Hummingbird Falls had weathered the storm. Ellie wondered if Colby and Rosie had weathered whatever storm they were caught in, too.

THIRTY-NINE

ROSIE ROLLED HER EYES as far as she could to the side, trying to see who was holding her down.

"Quiet, don't say a word. I'll let go, if you promise to stay still and not talk," whispered a familiar voice.

Rosie nodded her head yes and the hands let her go. She lay quietly and then turned her head toward her assaulter. It was Colby. Her heart beat faster and tears welled in her eyes. She longed to reach up and hug him.

But that feeling changed fast, as she thought about how much he had scared her. She opened her mouth to yell at him, to tell him to get his big heavy body off her back, when his hand swooped down over her mouth again. She glared at him, but nodded she understood and Colby slowly withdrew his hand.

This time she kept her mouth shut, turned all the way over and sat up. She stared at him. She placed her hand on his forehead, rubbed it over his crown and down his neck. She neither saw nor felt any injury. She was relieved there was no sign of blood. No cut. His hatless head looked just fine. She mouthed without sound, "Are you okay?"

Colby nodded yes. He stroked her cheek and smiled. Then he pointed toward the men. Short Man, who was walking away, stopped and turned to face Tall Man, who held the rifle on his shoulder, ready to fire.

"If you kill me, boss, you'll never find the money. You need me," Short Man yelled. "Beson whispered something just before he died. When I bent down to make sure he was dead, he told me where in the hut he hid the bag of money."

"You're lying, Bennie. He never said nothing. I was there."

"You just didn't hear it, boss. If you kill me, you'll have no idea where to look and no one to help you climb up there."

Colby pulled out his gun. He signaled Rosie to move to her left as he approached from the right. He held up his closed fist and then put out one finger at a time. On the count of five, they would start moving into position.

He handed Rosie her gun, which he had taken from her. She checked it. She stood up, looked at Colby and smiled. She made the okay sign with her gloved fingers. Then they moved in opposite directions, circling closer to the men who continued to argue.

"Can't you understand why I had to shoot Beson? When we were driving up here, you heard him say the FBI was getting closer, that he'd been under surveillance. He was close to cracking. You know he'd turn on us in a minute if it meant he could save his own skin."

"But he was the one with the money. What if he didn't hide it at the hut? He could've been stringing us along. Now we might never know where it is."

"Look, when I slashed him with the knife, he talked plenty to get me to stop. You saw it with your own eyes. He wasn't lying while he was bleeding all over the back of the truck and begging for his life. He was telling the truth about stashing the money in the hut. That was the original plan. After all, he knew the hut like the back of his hand. He'd been up there hundreds of times. It's a perfect hiding place."

Tall Man shifted in the snow, lowering his rifle a bit. "I think the big boss made a mistake letting him keep all the money. Kept us from being collared at the police barricade, but gave Beson too much power."

"Boss, Beson's not like us; he's just a stupid loan manager who got deep into debt by gambling. He'd never have robbed his bank if we didn't threaten him and his family. When he pulled that gun on us on the trail, I had to shoot him. Come on, boss. You know that."

The snow muffled the sound of Rosie and Colby as they made their way closer, but they were more noticeable than before. Visibility had increased as the blizzard let up. Now only a few last flakes were whirling their way to the ground. The last light before dusk turned peach-colored as Rosie turned and saw Colby was crawling closer, almost in position. She quickened her pace. When she was close enough and a large tree trunk protected her from the sight of the two men, she stood up and looked for Colby. She spotted him on the other side of the clearing. He was watching for her.

He saw her in position, raised his hand and then brought it down in a five count. When he reached five, he pointed his gun at the men and yelled, "Freeze. Police. Drop your weapons. Get down. Get down on the ground with your hands behind your back."

Rosie aimed her gun at the men as she stepped from behind the tree. "Don't try anything funny," she called. "We've got you surrounded."

"Oh, you think so?" a voice said, right behind Rosie.

FORTY

WHILE BONNIE WALKED to the town hall for her car, Ellie, Buddy and Millie stopped for a few minutes at the post office so Sarah could see Ellie for herself. The two friends hugged each other as best they could over the barrier of the counter. Sarah was strict about rules and didn't allow anyone behind the counter or into the post office interior unless they were part of the staff.

After making sure Ellie was alive and well, Sarah said, "Now you go make yourself to home. There's plenty to eat. Leftover chicken potpie in the refrigerator. Just warm it up in the microwave. Good thing we didn't lose the electricity in the storm. I was afraid of that. Oh, yes, there's shinbone soup and some crusty bread. If that doesn't interest you, just look in the freezer; take whatever you want. In the cupboard…"

"Whoa, Sarah," Ellie interrupted. "Don't worry. I know where everything is. I've been to your house so many times. You know me, I'll be settled in long before you're home from work. Besides, I'm not particularly hungry right now. We just came from the Pastry Shop. I brought you a blueberry pie." Ellie held up the white paper box with the Pastry Shop logo.

"Well, you'll have to eat it yourself. My doctor said I have to stay away from sweets until my triglycerides go down."

"I can't eat it. I'm full up with blueberries right now. Millie, how about you? Will you take the pie?"

"No, thanks. We get a lot of leftover food at the end of the evening from the chef at the inn. Why don't you just save it for later, Ellie? Those pastries seem to do you good. Look how you've rallied since you ate the turnovers."

"I think the coffee and caffeine probably helped, too. Oops, sorry, Geraldine. I'm blocking the way. Just go right ahead of me."

A large woman carrying a huge package pushed around Ellie to the counter. "Thanks. I'm kind of in a hurry. I've got to get this package mailed to my sister and then I'm planning to go to fire station and find out what Howie found. I heard at the town hall he and his crew got back from the woods with a body."

"A body?" Sarah exclaimed.

"That's my body," Ellie gasped. "I mean, I found it first and then called the police to tell them where to find it. Betsy said Howie would have to do the search because Dave, Colby and Rosie were up the notch, on some case. Turns out, Colby was missing and Dave went up to help Rosie find him. Anyway, it's a long story. Do they know who the body is—um, was?"

"I don't know. I heard from Debbie at the town hall that Howie won't say anything about it until Dave gets back. But the word is the body isn't anyone from town. Maybe it's a hunter from out of state."

"I'd like to go to the fire station, too. They may need to hear from me about when I saw him and what I figured happened. After all, I'm the one who discovered him."

"Now, Ellie," scolded Sarah. "What you need to do

is go to my house and rest. Put your overnight stuff in the guest room and if you want, just hop in bed and rest. Don't go running all over town. You've done more than enough for one day. I'll be home in an hour or so."

"I guess you're right. All this excitement's starting to wear me out. I'm really tired. But, if you hear anything, Geraldine, call Sarah so she can tell me when she gets home, will you?"

Before Geraldine could answer, Sarah spoke up again.

"My dear friends, I'm sorry, but we'll have to finish this conversation later, somewhere else. I need to keep the customers' line moving. This is a post office, you know. Federal business."

Ellie and Millie moved to the side and let Sarah wait on Geraldine.

"Thank you, Ellie. I'll see you later. Millie, thanks for helping Ellie out today. We needed you.

"Now Geraldine, I'll put your package on the scale. It's going to your sister Ida in New York, isn't it? How is she? Did she have her baby yet?"

Ellie and Millie waved goodbye to Sarah, who waved back and then turned to her business of processing Geraldine's package and procuring the update on the sister she had never met, but knew practically everything about. The post office was a veritable information vortex. Everyone came to the post office at some time and most gossiped freely with the inquisitive Miss Sarah about their lives and others'.

Bonnie was waiting in her car outside the post office when Millie and Ellie came out. She drove Millie up to the Hawk's Inn and then turned around to drive back into the village with Ellie.

MILLIE WALKED INTO the Hawk's Inn, where she worked as a server and her husband Todd tended bar. They would be busy tonight, for hordes of downhill and cross-country skiers, snowboarders, snowshoers and mushers with their teams of sled dogs would ignore the bad driving conditions and make their way to the mountains for the first snow of the year. They'd fill the hotels, inns and ski resorts. Tourists would jam restaurants, bars and gift stores. The village would transform from the orange of hunters to the multicolors of high-design skiwear overnight. Hummingbird Falls's businesses would make good money in the next few days.

Millie and Todd relied on crowds of eaters and drinkers and the tips they left. They were working hard to collect money to pay off the debts they had accrued in their past life. Both were committed to end their secrecy and come clean, pay off what they owed and start over. In their short time in Hummingbird Falls, they had learned wealth and material things were overrated. They discovered family, friends, community, honest work and safe living were what made life worthwhile.

Their oldest child, Matt, sixteen, was thriving. His teenage angst and suicidal thoughts had subsided, aided by the wonderful care and counseling James Foster provided him at the Foster's Home for Children, by the warm caring of the village residents and the constant love and attention from his mother and father.

Their daughter, Missy, had also changed. She no longer dreamed of morphing into a Paris Hilton–Brittany Spears sex star. Instead, she had replaced skimpy halter tops and tight miniskirts for athletic wear; she had taken up sports, joined the teen book club at the library and made some good friends.

Michael, eight, the youngest child, loved his new school, played on the soccer team and had a best friend he spent time with after school. He had joined the Cub Scouts.

Millie and Todd were so grateful. In spite of all the disaster their family had endured in their lives, they received a marvelous miracle, a gift, a chance for a new beginning and a better way of life. The village of Hummingbird Falls and its wonderful community had embraced them, unconditionally.

Millie shook her head in wonder as she removed her parka and walked into the huge dining room overlooking the golf course, now covered in bright white snow. The sun dipped below the mountains and the spectacle of the sunset was beginning.

BONNIE STOPPED HER CAR outside of Sarah's house. She helped Ellie with her overnight case as Ellie carefully carried the blueberry pie to the porch from the slippery sidewalk.

"I have to work for another hour to make up for the time I took off today. If you need anything before Sarah gets back, call. I can be here in a minute. You take care now."

Ellie gave Bonnie a hug, walked with Buddy up the stairs to Sarah's front porch and opened the door. In Hummingbird Falls, folks still left their doors unlocked, trusting their neighbors' honor and knowing their police cared about their safety.

Bonnie waved goodbye and then headed back to the town hall.

Ellie made herself comfortable in Sarah's house.

Her head was feeling better. She slipped into a sweat suit and she and Buddy cuddled down on the couch in front of the wood stove. Ellie was glad she was warm, safe and recovering from the events of this morning. She loved her wonderful, caring friends. The visit to the Pastry Shop was the cherry on her sundae, the frosting on her cake, and brought a smile to her face.

She was tired and looked forward to getting into her pajamas and going to bed, but she was going to wait until Sarah came home. She wanted to talk to Sarah about what happened today in Hummingbird Falls.

As Ellie nodded off in the warm comfort of Sarah's living room, she mused about the mystery of the body she found in the woods. How did it get there? Who was it? She remembered how the body looked. So waxen and unreal. The eyes so glazed and fixed.

She recalled seeing dead people at funerals. They looked staged. Their faces were covered with makeup, hair carefully coiffed and sprayed and bodies poised so unnaturally. The body she saw in the woods looked staged, too. Something wasn't right about it. It looked dead for sure, but somehow, it didn't seem like a live man who had died. More like a dummy, a pretend man, like she saw at the Ghoulog. In fact, just like the dummy she saw cut open by the evil surgeon.

Ellie sat straight up. That's where she knew that face. The body wasn't a dead man at all. It was a dummy made to look like a real man. It was the very same dummy she saw lying in an operating room in the haunted lodge at the Ghoulog. She remembered exactly how it looked.

She reached for Sarah's phone and dialed information. She asked for a number and copied it down on a scrap of paper. Then she dialed the number and waited until a male voice answered the phone.

"Dude, did you dump a body in the woods, recently?" she asked.

"What? Who's this? What body?" Dude asked.

FORTY-ONE

ROSIE TURNED TOWARD the voice. As she whirled around, the man grabbed her and pulled her against him. He twisted the gun out of her hand. When he placed his gun against her temple, she stopped struggling and put her hands up. A heavy-set man turned her around.

If the situation weren't so serious Rosie would have broken out laughing. Built like a wrestler gone to pot, garbed in an orange costume, which must have been his idea of hunter's gear, topped with a peaked orange hat, the man holding the gun on Rosie looked just like a pumpkin-person. His fat orange-red face, tipped at the bottom with a small goatee, held a mouth full of sharply pointed shark-like teeth. He was grinning like a jack-o'-lantern.

"Good girl. Do what you're told and we won't kill your friend."

Rosie glanced over at Colby. His hands were in the air, too, empty. No gun. A skinny man, dressed as a hunter, held a gun to his head. Seeing Colby in such a dangerous situation wiped all ideas of humor from her mind. She wished she could help him.

"Walk over there," pumpkin-man instructed Rosie, pointing to where Tall Man and Short Man had been arguing. They were now aiming their guns at Colby and Rosie, too, and had stopped yelling at each other. Rosie saw Colby and Skinny Man walking toward Tall and Short Man as well.

Colby glanced at Rosie when they got closer. "You okay?"

"Shut up. No talking," Skinny Man said as he swiped Colby's head with the gun butt.

Colby's head fell forward, but he didn't lose his balance. Blood trickled down through his sandy brown hair. He instinctively tried to cover his wound with his hands. Rosie gasped and stepped forward to help Colby. Pumpkin-man grabbed her and threw her down on the ground.

Skinny man ordered, "Don't move. Don't talk to him. Stay down there. Next time you won't just be pushed and he won't get a light knock on his head. You'll both get a bullet. Got it?"

Rosie nodded. She sat up, but made no move to stand. She looked at Colby. He looked pale, but was still standing. He gave her a little smile indicating he was okay. His hands were still on the crown of his head.

The four men moved to the side and talked in whispers. Rosie watched them, and then noticed the snow had stopped. A dim sun appeared. It was dropping toward the mountains and the red-peach of the sunset was merging into purple dusk.

Rosie took the opportunity to mouth a message to Colby.

"Are you all right?"

"Yeah, but my head hurts."

"He really whacked you."

"Just wait until I get a chance to whack him. You'll see what a whack is."

"What should we do?"

"Stay still for now."

"Can we jump them?"

"Not now, wait till we have a chance."

"Dave's coming. He's bringing some men with him."

"When?"

"Not sure. Soon, I hope."

Colby nodded. "Me, too."

"I could pretend I'm panicking, get their attention."

"No. Stay still."

"But, what are we going to do?"

"Wait. Too dangerous. Four to two."

"They'll shoot us."

"No, they won't. We'll make the first move. Watch me. When I think the time is right, I'll yell. You jump for the closest gun."

"What are you going to do?"

"Take out the skinny one. Then you take on the closest gun."

The mouthed conversation ended as the four men stopped whispering and turned toward Colby and Rosie.

Tall Man walked over to them. "You, down." He pushed Colby and Colby sank into the snow, as close to Rosie as he could get.

"Who else knows you're here?"

Colby and Rosie answered at the same time. Colby said, "No one." Rosie said, "My boss's coming any minute. He's got a lot of deputies with him."

Colby and Rosie stared at each other as Tall Man laughed and pointed the gun at Rosie's head. "I think the girl's telling the truth."

Short Man, who had been arguing earlier with Tall Man, spoke up. "See? I told you. We've got to get out of here fast. Shoot them now. They've seen us. We've got to get rid of them."

"No," said Pumpkin-man. "Don't kill them. Just knock them unconscious and leave them. We'll be long gone by the time they wake up or the cops ever find them. I don't want to be charged with murdering a cop."

"But they've seen us, Sully," Skinny Man whined.

"Shut up. No names, jerk," Tall Man said. "Look, what difference will it make to kill them? They wouldn't be the first ones we've knocked off and we can't take any chances. I say kill them and I'm the boss when the big boss isn't here. So, get rid of them now."

Skinny Man, who had captured Colby, took a step forward and aimed his gun at Colby. "I'll kill him first. One of you kill the girl."

The men looked at each other. "Well?" asked Tall Man.

"You do it," said Pumpkin-man. "I can't kill a woman."

Tall Man turned to curse out Pumpkin-man. Colby saw his chance. He yelled and leapt to his feet. He grabbed the rifle stock from the hand of Skinny Man, who was standing over him. Rosie jumped toward Tall Man and knocked his gun out of his hand and him into the snow, all the time screaming like a banshee. Pumpkin-man and Short Man pointed their guns at the moving bodies, but didn't dare shoot.

"Get clear. Let me get a shot," Short Man shouted. The wrestling couples continued their struggles, moving like tango dancers in snow parkas and boots. Then Tall Man managed to break free from Rosie.

"Shoot her, goddamn it. Now."

FORTY-TWO

BOB FOUND ANDY LYING in the snow by following the sound of his moans. As Bob made his way across the clearing toward Andy, he noticed the snow had almost stopped falling. Only a few flakes whirled here and there. He glanced at his watch. Almost 5:00 p.m. It was dark. Night had come while they were under the hemlock tree. "How are you, Andy? Are you hurt?"

"I'm not good. It got me. My hand. I can't move it."

"Oh, no. Let me see it."

"You'll need a flashlight. I dropped mine somewhere. My hand hurts a lot."

"I'll see what I can do about it. Have you seen Jim?"

"No. I thought he was right next to me, but when that crazy bear ran at us, I think Jim backed away fast. Call him."

"Jim. Jim. Answer me." There was no response. "I'm going to find a flashlight and look for Jim. You got your gun, Andy?"

"No, I left it under the tree, up against the trunk with my other stuff. I had a hard enough time getting myself out from under there. Even if I had a gun, I don't think I could use it. My right hand's hurt and I'm right-handed. I wouldn't be able to hold it, man, let alone aim. Do you think the bear's coming back?"

"I don't know. I think I hit it, but I'm not sure how

many times, or where. It must have smelled the food and followed us. Maybe it's hurt or scared enough so it won't come back. But, I wouldn't count on it. I've heard lots of bear stories. If this one's a rogue bear, then it'll probably come back to get revenge. If it's hungry, it might come back, thinking we have more food. I just don't know."

"What can we do?"

"I don't know. We have to take first things first. I'm going to find a flashlight, Jim and the first-aid kit. I have my Glock. If I hear the bear, I'll just aim in its direction and hope I hit it. Keep your eyes and ears open. Stay here. Don't move until I can see how bad your hand is. I'll be back."

"It's so dark now; I can't make out what's a tree trunk and what might be a bear. It could sneak up on us. Oh, God," said Andy, his voice shaky. "You're sure you don't see it?"

"Yeah, it's gone. I'm sure it ran off. We have to keep as quiet as we can so it doesn't hear us and come back. We want to be ready for it if it does. First, I'm going to get what I can find, then look at your hand. I've got to find Jim and see how he is. I should try to get a fire going. A big fire might keep the bear away. Aren't bears scared of fires?"

"Obviously, this one wasn't. Maybe he's rabid," Andy said.

"God, I didn't think about that. If you hear anything, yell. Don't move. I'll be right back."

Bob made his way toward the hemlock tree. Most of their equipment and the rifles were at the base of the tree, up against the trunk. If he could only get there before the bear came back, they might have a chance.

He walked, his ungloved hands freezing cold, reached the tree and crawled under it.

Bob's hands started to fumble over objects—a pan, a stick—and finally the roots of the tree leading to the trunk. Jim's backpack rested against the trunk, under a covering of snow, along with a day pack and the rifles. He hung one of the rifles over his shoulder. Inside Jim's pack he could feel clothes, a can of beer, a pack of gum, a pair of gloves and a small headlight. He slipped the gloves on, then the headlight and pressed the button. The small light popped on. Bob sighed in relief.

He pulled all the clothes from Jim's pack and stuffed them into his parka. Then he looked around.

Everywhere under the tree were signs of chaos. Huge paw marks indented the snow. Claws had ripped into everything edible and anything else around the fire holding food. Bob continued to dig through the snow piles. He found a flashlight and switched it on, too. Light helped make his task easier. He found the first-aid kit, fortunately, in one piece. He collected Jim's and Andy's parkas and walked back to Andy.

"Here, Andy. Put your parka on. I didn't find your hat. That hand looks bad, but it's not bleeding much."

"It hurts like hell."

"I know it must really hurt. Put some cloth over it, then snow. Pile these clothes on or under your legs. I've gotta look for Jim. I'll be back as soon as I can. Take the flashlight. And here's my gun. You should be able to use it left-handed if the bear comes back. Maybe the gun's noise will be enough to keep him off us."

Bob tromped around the clearing looking for Jim, using the headlight to illuminate the shadows. Finally, the light flashed on a prone body. It was Jim. Scratches marred his face in several places. His eyes were closed. His lips were pulled into a tight grimace.

"Jim. Jim. Can you hear me? It's Bob. Jim, wake up."

Jim didn't answer. He just lay in the snow, his glove-less hands almost blue with cold. Bob pulled off the gloves he was wearing and did his best to put them on Jim's hands. He covered Jim's upper body with his parka and put the rest of the extra clothes under his head and back to shield him from the cold snow.

He yelled, "Andy, I found Jim. He doesn't look good. He's unconscious. It'll take me a while to see what's going on with him. Then I'll look at your hand. In the mean-while, you've got to keep as warm as you can. The temperature's going to drop before we can get out of here."

"Okay." Jim could hardly hear Andy's faint voice. "Maybe I'll try to walk over to where you are. I'd feel safer with you two."

"Good idea, if you can. Safety in numbers and we wouldn't have to yell."

Bob turned back to Jim. As Bob scanned his body with the head light, he saw Jim's right leg was bent at an odd angle.

"I'm going to try to make Jim more comfortable. Where are you, Andy? Are you coming over here?"

Andy managed to get the parka on one arm. He held the flashlight with his left hand. The gun and his injured hand rested on his leg. The bear's claw had ripped the skin off his hand and it hung down, loose and bloody.

"I can't move my hand, Bob. It looks awful, and I can hardly stand the pain. I don't think I can get up, let alone make it over there. If the bear comes back, I won't be able to help. What're we going to do?"

Andy's voice broke and Bob yelled, "Don't worry.

We'll be okay. I've got my rifle right here, hanging on my shoulder. It's loaded and ready. If that monster comes back, he's dead. I'll be back soon. You just hold on."

"I'll try, but I'm scared, Bob. And the pain's making me dizzy. Hurry, will you?"

"Fast as I can, man. Just hold on."

Bob turned back to Jim and checked his pulse. It seemed to be okay. At least it was throbbing in his neck. "Jim, can you hear me?" No answer. No movement. Jim lay as if dead.

Bob moved his hands over Jim's body, feeling for injuries. The flashlight illuminated Jim's orange fleece vest, his checked flannel shirt and his blue jeans. Then Bob focused on the awkwardly placed right leg. The magnitude of the problem he faced sunk in. Sticking through the bloody lower-right pant leg was a white bone.

"Oh, my God."

Jim moaned. "It's okay, Jim. I'll try to fix you up. Just a broken bone. You'll be fine."

Bob didn't lie to himself, though. He murmured, "This's awful. How'll we ever get out of here? Jim can't walk and Andy can't help me drag or carry him. We've got no fire. No one knows where we are. There's a huge hungry bear out there probably waiting to kill us, and I have no idea which way's closest to help."

Bob calmed himself down as best he could. "First things first," he whispered as he opened the first-aid kit and studied the contents. "Thank goodness I bought the best at L.L. Bean. There's even an instruction booklet."

Bob thumbed through the pamphlet until he came to broken bones. He needed a splint, tightly wrapped, but not circulation-stopping. He had to keep Jim's leg immobile.

He continued talking to himself in whispers. "Well, sticks would do for a splint. The ace bandage works for wrapping it together. But keeping motionless means Jim has to stay put. Either Andy, if he isn't too badly injured, or I have to try to find help. One of us has to stay with Jim."

He looked up with a prayer. He hoped God was watching out for them. It was then he saw the stars. Even the occasional snowflakes had stopped falling and the sky was ablaze with diamond chips.

"One piece of good news, at least. Other hunters will be out first thing in the morning with the good weather. We'll holler, shoot off our guns. Someone's bound to find us."

He sent a message of gratitude toward the stars. He remembered the old saying, "It's only in the dark you can see the stars."

With a little more hope, he began crawling around looking for branches to use for a splint. It was a blessing Jim was unconscious. He knew Jim's leg would hurt like hell when he moved it and wrapped it.

Bob found some branches for the splint and then walked over to the small circle of light Andy's flashlight made. He pointed his headlight toward Andy and found him lying down, his eyes closed.

"I'm glad you're taking it easy, Andy. That's the best thing to do right now. Rest. Jim's unconscious. He's got a bone sticking out of his leg. I have to figure out how to splint him so I can move him to a safer place."

Andy opened his eyes and sobbed, "I never had a

chance to shoot at that damn thing. I was too surprised to know what was happening. The snow fell on us and then it came charging in. All I wanted to do was run."

"I know. Me, too."

"It didn't get me until after it was shot. When it ran out, it jumped right on me. Took my hand. I don't know whether it bit me or clawed me. It hurts so much."

"I'll see what I can do for your hand when I finish with Jim. Can you crawl in under the hemlock tree? It might be safer and warmer under there. At least if the bear comes back, he'd have to attack from the front. We'd have a little protection against the tree trunk. If you can make it over there, you can check on the coals from the fire. Maybe some of them are still warm and you can dig them out and start up another fire. Maybe you could look for another flashlight, food, something to use as weapons, anything."

Bob was desperate. He couldn't allow Andy to fall apart. He needed him to listen for the bear, to help him figure out what to do. He couldn't take care of both Jim and Andy. Since Andy was least hurt, he needed to snap out of his trauma and start taking some action.

"Come on, Andy, you can do it. I'll help you. You don't want to be caught out here in the clear if the bear comes back, do you?"

Andy got on his knees and holding the flashlight and gun in one hand, leaned on Bob's arm. Andy's other hand hung useless by his side.

Slowly the two hunters pushed their way through the deep snow toward the hemlock tree.

"As soon as I get you settled, Andy, I have to go back to Jim. He's in bad trouble, I think. You'll be okay here by yourself for a while."

Andy tried to rally. He sat down near a pile of snow and with his good hand started pawing through it.

"You do what you have to, Bob. I'll try to find some stuff to help. I wish it wasn't so cold. I wish I was home. Oh, God, Bob, I wish I were a hundred miles away from here."

FORTY-THREE

DAVE, REGGIE, MIKE and the dogs moved as fast as they could as they climbed up the trail. The snow began to let up some, and the late-afternoon sun lit up the landscape for a while before setting quickly behind the mountain. The last hints of light colored the clouds overhead mauve and light lavender.

After another half hour of rigorous hiking, Dave signaled them to stop for a break. They drank coffee and finished the sandwiches and cookies. As they sat quietly without talking, the last few snowflakes fell and the wind died. The white world stilled. They could hear nothing but the sound of their breath huffing in the thin air. It was as if they were the only ones alive up here.

Then Dave heard something. The others did, too. Not too far off, the sound of voices drifted through the trees.

"That's got to be them. No one else would be up here in this weather."

"What should we do?" Reggie asked.

"We'll head toward the voices. Keep very quiet. No talking. Get your guns ready, just in case. I hope we can tell from the sound whose voices they are. If it's Rosie and Colby, then good.

"When we get close enough, if I see trouble, I'll put

my hand up in the air. Stop. When I signal go, move in as fast as possible, guns ready. Okay?"

The men nodded. Reggie asked, "Do you think they're in bad trouble? Like someone's hurt them?"

"I don't know. I hope not. We could catch up to them and find they're fine. But I have a feeling something bad's going on. We already have one dead body. Let's pray we don't find any more. We've got to be careful. Don't shoot until I say so. Rosie and Colby could be close to other people. We sure don't want to be careless and shoot innocent folks. Enough said. Let's go. Watch me. If I say shoot, then take aim and shoot. But only if I say so."

Mike tied the dogs to a tree and Dave led the way up the trail toward the voices. The sound of talking grew as they moved closer. They came around a curve in the trail. Dave signaled for them to stop. He pointed to disturbed snow leading into the woods. With hand gestures he motioned he was going to follow that path into the woods. The others nodded and watched Dave trudge into the timber.

Dave moved slowly and cautiously. Although the snow muffled his footsteps, he wanted to make sure nothing gave his presence away. He moved from tree to tree, closer and closer to the voices. He checked back to make sure he was still visible to the two men waiting on the trail. Two more trees, then he peered out into a small clearing.

Colby and Rosie were lying on the ground, motionless. Four men stood around them, guns in hand, arguing. A chill shivered Dave as he looked at this deadly scene and watched for any sign of life from his two deputies.

Dave didn't dare wait too long. Who knew what would happen? If Rosie and Colby were alive, but injured, waiting could be dangerous. If he waited too long, the men might kill them, slip away into the woods, and escape capture. If Colby and Rosie were already dead, he needed to move now to seize their murderers.

He raised the hand holding the gun high in the air. Reggie and Mike raised their hands in return and started toward him. When they were close enough, Dave put his hand out and stopped them. He pointed toward the clearing and put four fingers up, indicating four men. He bent over, signaling they needed to keep low. He held his gun out, showing them they needed to be ready to shoot. Mike and Reggie nodded in agreement. Even though they were not experienced gun fighters or law enforcement, they believed in Dave and were ready to follow him.

The three men crept closer to the clearing, hiding behind trees and keeping low. When Dave gave the signal, they ran into the clearing with their guns out.

Dave called, "Freeze. Put your guns down. We're the police."

The four men standing around Rosie and Colby's bodies looked up, startled. Pumpkin-man dropped his gun, Skinny Man put his arms over his head and Short Man ran. Tall Man, the boss, pulled Rosie to her feet and held his gun to her head.

"It's me or her, man. Which do you want?"

FORTY-FOUR

THE THREE NEW JERSEY hunters huddled under the hemlock tree. Bob was unable to restart their fire, but had found some crackers in a tin the bear somehow missed. Bob managed to wrap Jim's broken leg, drag him under the tree, and wrap him in all the extra clothes he could find. Andy fed Jim crackers and the last beer. Soon Jim closed his eyes, pain moving him to an unconscious state again.

Bob examined Andy's hand and was relieved the wounds didn't seem life-threatening. He wrapped the hand carefully and Andy was working hard to overcome his pain and misery.

Now the two injured hunters slept, while Bob sat up, gun in hand, watching out for the bear and thinking. He decided he would have to go for help. Jim could not move and someone had to stay with him in case the bear returned. In this cold weather, without fire and badly injured, it was only a matter of time before death hunted you down. Bob had to find his way to civilization. His hunt was now for people and help.

He studied his compass. He planned to head south, moving downhill, and hoped to meet some hunters. He would leave at dawn.

FORTY-FIVE

DAVE DIDN'T STOP TO THINK. He took careful aim and shot Tall Man in the head, which was a good five inches above Rosie's hat. Both Rosie and Tall Man fell into the snow. Dave ran over to check Rosie. Colby jumped to his feet when Tall Man fell and was running after Short Man, who dashed into the woods. Reggie and Mike ran into the clearing, picked up the dropped guns, pushed the other two men down on the snow and handcuffed them together with Dave's cuffs. By the time they were finished, Colby walked back into the clearing, hauling the man who had tried to run off.

Dave bent over Rosie. He turned her body over, holding his breath. She smiled at him, tears running down her face, and then wrapped him in a big hug.

"My hero," she gasped. "What a shot, boss. I could feel its heat as it singed my hair. I'm lucky you didn't blink."

Dave laughed. "Glad you liked it. I know you're a better shot than me on the firing range, but when it counts, I can still draw a bead. Thank goodness."

Dave, Rosie and Colby patted three men down and relieved them of their identifications. Then they searched the pockets of the dead man.

"Looks like we have some Massachusetts criminals without valid licenses," Colby said.

"This name sounds familiar. Bonzeni. Isn't he one of the henchmen for the warehouse mob down in Boston?"

"I think you're right," said Rosie. "I thought I recognized him, but in the hunter's orange instead of jail stripes, I wasn't sure."

Dave said, "I bet the rest of them are mob, too. Hey, Bonzeni, who's the dead man?"

Bonzeni just stared at him. "I want to talk with my lawyer."

"All right. If that's the way you want it. We'll Mirandize you right here and then we're going to hike back down the trail straight to jail. Mike, you go on ahead. Take Colby's car keys. Use the radio and call Betsy. Tell her what's going on and that we need the FBI agent from Greenberg to meet us at police headquarters. Tell her we're bringing in three mobsters who allegedly murdered a man, kidnapped two police officers and threatened deadly harm. Tell her to contact Doc Muller and inform him we'll need him up here first thing in the morning. We have two more corpses for him."

"I'm on my way," Mike said, taking Colby's keys. "Be careful. Even handcuffed, these guys are pretty scary."

Colby and Rosie lined up the three men and pushed them toward the trail. Reggie led them and Colby and Rosie followed close behind. Dave stepped back and bent over the man he had shot. He gently pulled the tall man's scarf up to cover his bloody head. "Sorry, fellow. Didn't want to have to kill you. Sleep well."

Then Dave started the long hike back to the parking lot, in the growing darkness, thinking he would add in his bimonthly report to the selectmen that he investigated three suspicious deaths. That would get their attention.

As he trudged along, he sent his gratitude up to the first stars just starting to show in the skies. He gave his thanks to the universe. He and his two deputies, his friends, were alive and safe. This fall hunt had ended successfully.

FORTY-SIX

ROSIE AND COLBY CHATTED and slowly made their way
down the trail, following the handcuffed robbers.

"Sure glad you found me. It wasn't any fun being up
here all by myself," Colby said.

"Tell me about it," Rosie shot back. "When I
dropped the two-way, I felt like I was cut off from
everyone. No one could help me. What happened to
you, anyway? The last we heard from you was that
broken-up cell message early this morning. Why didn't
you call us back? We were worried to death."

"Hey, don't be angry. It wasn't my fault. I would've
called if I could, believe me."

"Would've, could've, should've. The point is you
didn't call. Why not? Why didn't you call from your
radiophone in the car?"

"It's a long story."

"I don't care. It's a long way down. Tell me. I've
been a wreck all day, not knowing where you were or
what was happening. You owe me that much."

"Wait. Give me a chance. I'm sorry you and Dave
worried about me. I'm sorry I upset you. I know how
it is to worry about someone and not know if they're
okay." Colby paused. "It just went down that way. Wait
till you hear the whole story."

"Sorry," Rosie said. "I didn't mean to bark at you.

I'm not really mad, just so relieved you're all right. Words just come streaming out of my mouth when I'm upset. My dad used to say it's the Irish in me. Getting all worked up. Go on, I'm listening."

"Well, I pulled in Wilson's Folly lot shortly after nine. There were several cars and trucks parked. Two New Hampshire trucks, I recall, a couple of New York cars, a Massachusetts SUV and that New Jersey black Dodge Ram."

"Interesting. When I got there, only the two New Hampshire trucks and the Ram were there, along with yours."

"The other hunters must have left after I went up the trail."

"Did you look in the Ram?"

"Yep. First I checked out the other vehicles and they were all legal, stickers up-to-date and parked fine. No tickets. Then I drove over to the Ram. I had a funny feeling about it, so I parked so it couldn't leave without going through my SUV."

"What tipped you off?"

"I'm not sure. The truck was too clean; the license was too new. I don't know. It just didn't look like a truck a hunter would have. No gun racks, no NRA stickers."

"So then what?"

"I looked inside. Saw the blood. Knew there was trouble. Saw a trace of blood leading to the trail and followed it. Read the sign-up sheet. That didn't help me, so I started up the trail, to find out what happened."

"Why didn't you call then?"

"Just as I reached the trail, I heard a scream for help. No time to call in then." Colby paused while the group ahead negotiated a difficult part of the trail. When they successfully made it through, he continued.

"I was running up the trail. Didn't see anyone. The screaming had stopped by then. I wasn't sure what was happening, so kept real quiet and got off the trail, stayed hidden behind trees. About ten minutes later, I checked the trail itself. The blood drippings had stopped. So I backtracked to the last trace of blood I could find, looking on both sides of the trail. Didn't find any at all. Didn't know whether they had gone on, or back, or off trail, or if the bleeding had just stopped. That's when I called Dave."

"Your call broke up."

"Yeah, I know. Must have been out of range. I thought about going back to the SUV, but decided I'd better keep going, trying to find out who was bleeding and what was happening first. I knew Dave would figure out where I called from and follow up."

"I found your hat. It had blood on it."

"Good. I hoped someone would find it. I rubbed my hat on the last drops of blood I could find. I wanted to make sure we had a DNA sample. Did you read the note?"

"What note? I didn't find any note."

"Damn. I wrote a note saying I was following someone who might be hurt badly, that the hat had a DNA sample on it, wrote down the New Jersey license, in case the vehicle had left while I was up trail, and the time. You didn't get it when you picked the hat off the tree?"

"The hat was buried under snow on the trail. There wasn't any note."

"I put the note in the hat, pushed it onto a branch next to the trail. I knew you and Dave would recognize my hat."

"I was lucky to find it at all. When I found the blood, I thought you'd been hurt. I called Dave and told him he had to come up with a crew and help me find you."

"No wonder you were so scared. Oh, boy, that sure backfired. I'm sorry. I couldn't think of any other way to get information to you. I rushed off so fast; I left my two-way in the back of the SUV. I didn't dare take the time to go back and get it."

"No wonder I couldn't get hold of you. I reached Stan all the way up at the hut, but couldn't get you. That really worried me. I didn't understand why you didn't answer. I thought you were hurt or..." Rosie didn't finish her sentence.

They hiked a while in silence. Then Rosie said, "I messed up, too. I left my two-way next to the dead man on the trail. Totally forgot I took it off my belt. I walked off without it. Dave must've been wild when he couldn't get either you or me. We'll have to sit through a long lecture about that when we get back."

The two friends laughed. They moved a little closer to each other after that.

"The rest of the story's pretty tame. I just kept hiking up off trail. After it started to snow, every so often, I'd spot footsteps. I guessed there were at least five people, so I kept my distance. I hoped you or Dave would catch up. And then you showed up."

"Wait a minute. What about the dead man? Did you see him?"

"Actually, no. I heard a gun shot. I didn't know if a hunter had shot a deer or if the people I was following fired a gun. I tried to pick up my speed, but walking off trail's hard. Slowed me down. But it was better than being spotted by them, especially as the odds were five-to-one. Somehow, I missed the dead guy altogether. I'd hike off one side of the trail and then switch to the other side. I must have passed him when I was on the opposite side."

"I wasn't moving very fast. How'd I catch up to you?"

"Probably because they stopped. That's when I caught up with them. They were fighting, arguing about what to do. They must have split up because when I first spotted them, only two men were in that clearing, still arguing. I knew three more were somewhere. At the time, I didn't know one of them was dead. Then I saw you."

"And scared me to death. Did you have to jump so hard? Couldn't you have said who you were?"

"Couldn't take the chance, sorry. I didn't want you to yell. Because of the odds, we needed to come out as a complete surprise to them."

"Well, I understand and I'd already forgiven you for it," Rosie laughed again. "You know you're going to have to go over the whole thing again for Dave?"

"Yep. And you'll have to tell him every move you made, too. We'll probably be writing reports all night."

"Maybe you can come over to my apartment and have a few beers with me while we write them," Rosie suggested.

"Sounds good to me," Colby answered with a big smile.

FORTY-SEVEN

SARAH BANGED THE DOOR behind her. Ellie and Buddy jumped, opening their eyes wide and turning toward the door.

"Oh, it's only you," Ellie said.

"Well, that's a nice way to greet me," Sarah answered as she hung up her coat and worked her boots off. "Hello to you, too."

"You know what I meant. I thought for a moment it might be a murderer or a monster. I guess I fell asleep. I was dreaming about those awful creatures from the Ghoulog."

"Well, I'm not any of those bad things. Just a tired out old postmistress. I caught the weather report on my way home. Can you believe the temperature's actually rising? The meteorologist says it's going to be fifty degrees tomorrow."

"Wow. All this snow's going to melt. The brooks'll be roaring. In fact, I think I can hear the falls now."

"Yep, they're running so fast with melting snow, they're practically all white water and pushing at the banks. I hope we don't flood like last spring, or was it the spring before? Time seems to move so fast sometimes."

Sarah sighed, walked into the kitchen, and washed her hands. She started taking food out of the refrigerator.

"Want a glass of wine while I warm up the shin-bone soup?"

"Sounds lovely. Can I help?"

"No. You rest. How's your head?"

"Better. Much better. In fact, it hardly hurts at all. Only when I touch it."

"Good. I was worried there for a while."

"Me, too. But I guess it takes more than a tree limb and a rock to crack my thick skull."

"I'm glad you said that and not me, Ellie. You'd be on me in a second if I made any comment about your thickness or your head."

The two women laughed. Sarah rustled around in the kitchen for a moment and then walked back out carrying a tray with two glasses of red wine and a plate with crackers and sliced cheese.

"The soup and bread are warming, so I'll just relax with you while we're waiting. Reggie swore this is a good-tasting wine. The cheese is Irish cheddar. If you don't like it, take it up with Reggie."

Ellie took a sip of wine and then munched a cracker loaded with two slices of cheese. "Umm, good. No complaints from me."

"Rarely do you complain when the subject's food. But tell me everything. You've had quite a day. Give me all the details."

Ellie proceeded to fill Sarah in chronologically from early this morning, ending with her call to Dude.

"So you called Dude? What did he say? Did you talk to his brother Oman?"

"No, just Dude. He was shocked. You know, he's such a nice young man. And so tall and handsome."

"I know what he looks like. What did he say?"

"He said he didn't know anything about a body or a dummy in the woods. The one they were using for the Ghoulog was specially altered so when the actor playing the surgeon pressed a button, the alien would jump out of the stomach cavity. Each time a group passed through, the actor would pop the alien back in and cover it with intestines they got from Steve, the guy who butchers deer. I guess he dresses out domestic animals, too."

"What's that got to do with anything? Get to the point, please."

"Dude told me they can only use the guts for so long before they smell too bad, so they had been taking the rotting guts to the dump like every other day. But by the end of the Ghoulog, just a week ago, the dummy smelled so foul they decided they couldn't pack it up, or use it again next year. He asked one of the volunteers to take it to the dump."

"So, how did it get into the woods?"

"Well, he didn't know. He's going to talk to the volunteer and his brother and find out if they know anything about it. Dude was so sorry. He kept apologizing for upsetting me and for all the trouble Howie and the volunteers had to go through. Especially in the middle of the squall."

"He should be sorry. I know he's still young and means well, but you can't just dispose of a smelly old carcass in the woods, like that. What was the guy thinking of?"

"If Dude can't find out, then I will. At least I think I can solve that mystery. It seems I'm left out of all the rest. Did you hear any more about Dave? Are Rosie and Colby all right?"

"No. Didn't hear a thing. But I want to know. I'm going to call Betsy and see what's going on."

Sarah reached for the phone and called the police department. A male voice answered.

"This is Sarah. I'm calling for Dave."

"Hello, Ms. Sarah. Dave isn't here. But we just got a radio message he'll be here in about an hour. Can I help you? It's Bobby."

"Is everything okay? Did he find Colby and Rosie?"

"As I understand it, the mission was a success. They're bringing back three criminals from Massachusetts and left two dead behind for the Doc."

"Oh, my goodness. The two dead aren't ours, are they?"

"No, all of us are just fine. I don't know any more details. Can I have Dave call you later?"

"That won't be necessary. He'll have a lot to do, I imagine. I'll just wait for tomorrow and talk to him then. Thanks, Bobby."

Sarah hung up the phone and relayed the conversation to Ellie, who sat with a gaping mouth while she listened. Then both women emptied their wineglasses.

"I'll get us some more wine. The soup and bread should be ready. Do you want a salad?"

"Soup and bread's enough, thanks."

"You stay on the couch. I'll bring the food in here. We'll eat on trays in front of the fire."

"That's nice. Sarah," Ellie called into the kitchen, "what do you think about those criminals who were captured? What do you think they were doing climbing up the trail?"

"Don't know. They're not the sort to be having fun in the wilderness."

"You're right. They must have been after something. Let me think."

Sarah carried a tray with a bowl of soup, a plate of bread and butter, and another glass of wine to Ellie. She went back into the kitchen and returned with an identical tray for herself.

"Let's figure it out," she said, raising her glass to Ellie.

Ellie clinked her wineglass against Sarah's. "To figuring this mystery out," she said. "Now, why would those men be climbing that trail?"

"Same reason the chickens crossed the road, or the bears went over the mountain, I assume," answered Sarah as she buttered her bread. "To get to the other side. To see what they could see."

"Sarah. You're brilliant. That's it. They were climbing to get somewhere. And Wilson's trail, as I remember, doesn't go to the other side, or across a road. It goes straight to the top, to the climbers' hut on the top."

"Yep. You're right. That old hut up there is the only destination they could head for, unless they were going for the views. I doubt they're the types who would do all that climbing for a view."

"So they were climbing to the hut. For what reason? What would criminals from out of state want with a climbers' hut?"

"To hide out?"

"There are lots easier places to hide out than at the top of a difficult climbing trail. Why did they pick that place in particular?"

"Hmm. I guess that's the million-dollar question."

"You did it again, Sarah. Wow, you're clever. A

million dollars. The Greenberg Federal Bank! Those robbers stole over a million dollars."

"That was months ago. I know they got away with a new delivery of fifty-dollar bills. It's a federal crime. I get notices of all federal crimes in this area to post for the general public, like wanted posters."

"Well, what if they were looking for the money?"

"Why would they be looking for the money up on the mountain now, when they stole it a couple of months ago?"

"That's a good question. I'll have to think more on it."

"While you're thinking, I'm going to do up these dishes and then get my pj's on. I'm reading a great book. *Grave Secrets,* a romantic suspense by Dixie Land. You've read some of her books, haven't you?"

"Yes, I loved *Exit Wounds* and *Circle of Secrets.* You go ahead. I think I'll just get in bed and write a little. I'm feeling very full, comfy and sleepy. I'll probably doze off."

"You sleep as late as you want. Give me a call when you wake. What are your plans for tomorrow?"

"I have to call Carmen, down at the walk-in clinic, and tell her I'm better. Then, I want to stop over at the police station, see what's going on, tell Dave what Dude told me and throw out our theory as to why those men were on the Wilson trail. Then I'll find a ride home from someone who isn't too busy. I know you're tied up."

"At least until noon, when we close for an hour. If you wait till then, I could take you."

"No, I want to get back home before then. I have lots to do. Thanks for having me tonight, Sarah, especially on such short notice. I appreciate it."

"Oh, don't be silly. You'd do the same for me. Go get in bed now. I'll finish up here, let Buddy out one more time and get in bed myself. You know I have to get up early for work, get the flag up, sort the new mail and open the doors by 8:00 a.m."

"You work too hard, Sarah. Why don't you retire?"

"And do what? I don't want to retire. I hope I die sorting mail. I have such a great job. I get to keep up with everyone. Know what's going on. Never a dull day. Night now, Ellie. No more talk of retiring. It seems to work for you, but it's not my cup of tea. Speaking of tea, do you want some Sleepytime Tea? I always brew a cup before bed."

"That would be wonderful. Thanks."

Ellie patted her sleeping dog, walked into the guest room and snuggled under the red-checkered quilt. She remembered Sarah coming in with a cup of tea, Buddy jumping up on the bed, twirling around twice to find just the right spot to lie down, but she remembered nothing at all after that.

FORTY-EIGHT

ELLIE WOKE UP WITH A START. She sat up and stared straight ahead. Then she grabbed the pen and pad of paper from the nightstand and started drawing and scribbling as fast as she could.

After a few minutes, she paused, looked at what she had written and drawn and squeezed her eyes shut and sat motionless.

Then she whooped, jumped out of bed and danced around the room. Buddy joined her, barking and jumping up on her. She grabbed him and they danced together.

"Buddy, I've got it. I remembered. I dreamed what I forgot. I know what I saw."

She put Buddy down and spun around in circles. "I feel so happy. So free. Oh, my golly, it's finally over. I've remembered. My brain's back in order. I've got to get dressed and go see Dave right away."

After a quick breakfast of toast and jam, a couple of soft-boiled eggs and enough coffee to wash it all down, Ellie and Buddy headed out of doors. The sun's warmth was melting the sparkling snow.

Sidewalk gutters were little brooks, full with rushing snowmelt. In places green grass poked through the fast-disappearing white cover. As she walked, Ellie saw skis, poles, snowshoes and shovels leaning against neighbors' front porches and remains of snow sculptures dwindling in the warming air.

Ellie removed her hat and gloves and stuck them in her coat pocket. She unzipped her red parka. In no time at all, she was unbuttoning her wool sweater and wishing she didn't have on a turtleneck and her winter underwear. She had dressed in layers yesterday, but today was a different story.

It looked like the forecast was right this time. She stopped, turned her face up to the sun and closed her eyes. She breathed in the fresh air and smiled at the warmth she could feel on her face. Maybe the sun would put a little color back on her face. She, like others in this area, paled to a chalky white during winter, especially those who didn't spend hours on the ski slopes or in the tanning beds at the resort spas. Neither of these two activities interested Ellie in the least.

Ellie was walking to the town hall, which housed the police station in its basement. She passed the little church and the library, walked over the stone bridge and a few blocks past the frozen fishing pond in the park. She had to keep herself from skipping with joy. She couldn't wait to talk with Dave about what had she had discovered.

She arrived at the town hall just as a car dropped off a scraggy-looking hunter, holding a rifle, who ran to the glass door of the police station and pushed his way inside. She followed closely behind. He stopped by the dispatcher's desk and yelled at Betsy.

"Help me. Please help. My friends are hurt and lost up in the woods. A bear attacked us last night. I need help."

Dave rushed into the foyer, closely followed by

Rosie and Colby, who sported a white bandage on the crown of his head. They crowded around the hunter.

"Please remove any weapons you're carrying immediately and place them on the floor," Dave demanded.

The hunter looked bewildered. "What? I've been walking for hours. My friends need help. They're hurt."

"No weapons are allowed in here, except by the officers. Put your rifle and any other weapons you have on the floor and then we'll listen to your story." Dave stood up tall and puffed out his chest. He looked very commanding.

Bob placed his rifle on the floor, then grabbed his hunting knife and dropped it with a clatter. He searched his broad belt until he found his all-in-one handyman tool and flung that on the floor, too.

"Okay. Will you listen now, or do you want to frisk me and do a body-cavity search?"

"Take it easy, mister. It's nothing personal. Just regulations. No need for a body search, if you haven't any other weapons. Now, what's going on?"

Then Dave noticed Ellie, standing near the front door. "Hi, Ellie. Come on over. You don't have to stand way over there. Good to see you. I heard you had quite a day yourself yesterday. How's your head?"

Before Ellie could answer, the hunter yelled, "What is this? Old home day? Aren't you the police? What kind of loony bin have I walked into? I told you I've got an emergency and you ignore me and gossip with an old woman. What do I have to do? They might die out there."

"First thing you've got to do is watch your mouth," Colby said as he took a step closer to the hunter. "I don't like your attitude. And this woman's a lady and she deserves respect."

"I'm sorry. Let me start again. My name's Bob Scianni. My friends Andy and Jim are up the mountain somewhere. We got lost in the storm yesterday. They're hurt. A broken leg and a bad hand. A bear got them. I've walked for hours, finally found my way out and managed to thumb a ride down here. You've got to help me."

"Don't worry. We're on it. Betsy, call the mountain rescue squad and the search and rescue crew. Tell them we've got an emergency, lost and injured hunters, and need help immediately. We'll call them back with map coordinates when we get them."

"Right away, Chief," Betsy said, picking up the phone as she spoke.

"Now you—Bob, is it? Come into my office. Let's look at the map and see where your friends are."

"That's just it. I don't know. We got lost."

"We'll look at the map, find where you went in and estimate how far you might have gone. The helicopter won't have any trouble flying today and may be able to hunt them down, if we can narrow the search area. The sooner we get an idea of where you were, the sooner we can rescue your friends. Where did you exit the woods? We can put someone on your trail there and backtrack."

"I stumbled out by a river. It was running pretty fast. I found a small bridge, crossed it and came out on the highway, Route 46, I think. I stood in the middle of the road, ready to flag down a car. One came toward me, slowing down. I jumped in front of it, waving my hands. The man slowed some more, but didn't want to stop. So I grabbed the door as he pulled around me and jumped in anyway. He was mad, cursed at me a lot, but kept driving. He said he was in a hurry, but he'd drop me outside the police station. We passed some sign with the name of a falls on it. I forget the name—Emerald, Green, I don't know. It took us about fifteen minutes to get here."

"Where's the driver of the car? He could probably pinpoint the exact spot he picked you up."

"He kept saying he was in a hurry, didn't want to get involved. Had to be down south in an hour. Something like that."

"I saw the car, a dark blue Buick, newish model. License number ELT 4658, Massachusetts plates. A man about fortysomething with dark hair and a checkered cap was driving," Ellie inserted. "He pulled out fast after this gentleman jumped out."

All faces turned toward Ellie. She smiled. "It's just my nature, that's all. I notice things."

Colby whistled and turned to the hunter. "That's just one of the reasons to respect this lady, sir."

"Ellie, take one of Betsy's pens and write down that license number on a piece of paper. Colby, while she's doing that, grab your coat. I want you to find the driver that picked Bob up. He couldn't have gotten too far. Put your lights on and move it. Bring him back. Arrest him if you have to. Time's important here and he'll know where he picked Bob up. We need him to point out the location on the map."

"Got it, Chief. On my way." Colby grabbed his coat, the piece of paper Ellie handed him and ran out of the station. He started the police SUV, put the blue lights and siren on and took off fast.

Then the rest of the contingent, minus Betsy, who was talking on the phone, trooped into Dave's office. He pulled a map out of his desk drawer and spread it open on the top of the desk, covering reports, an apple core, his empty coffee cup and a myriad of other objects.

"Here's where we are," Dave said, pointing at a spot on the map. "Here's where Route 46 goes north of here."

The hunter watched as Dave traced his finger along a red curving line.

"Now, where did you leave your car?"

The hunter bent over the map. "We parked in a lot called Dalia's Place. Some man in a bar told us there were a lot of deer around there."

"And then?"

"Then we walked up a trail and then perpendicular to the trail, I think for about three hours. Stopped to cook breakfast. Then headed farther up hill."

"Okay, you're doing good. Here's Dalia's Place parking. See? This dotted line is the trail. Three hours would get you about here."

Dave used a pencil to draw the path the hunters most likely took.

"That look about right?"

Bob nodded.

"Then what?" Dave asked.

"Then it started to snow and we got lost. Couldn't see two feet in front of us. Got twisted around, our cells didn't work, and it was freezing. When we decided to turn back, we didn't know which way we'd come from. Chose downhill, hoping to catch the trail somewhere."

"Did you have a compass? Did you go north, south, east or west?"

"Sorry, I don't know. We had a compass and I tried to head south, but sometimes the terrain was too rocky and we had to turn in another direction. When the wind blew the heavy snow, you couldn't see anything. It was impossible to figure out which way to go."

"Well, we have a start anyway. Rosie, tell Betsy what you heard and have her relay it to rescue crews. One crew should start at Dalia's Place and follow the trail the hunters took. The other crew should look along Route 46 and see if they can find Bob's footsteps coming out of the woods. They could backtrack."

Rosie ran out of the room.

"If Colby finds the driver it'll save us a lot of time trying to find your footprints."

Rosie returned. "Another thing, Rosie. I want the helicopter to circle the area around Dalia's Place. Maybe they can spot them from the air."

Rosie left the room again.

"Bob, I want you to sit down on that chair and breathe. You didn't get hurt, did you?"

"No. But I'm pretty shaken up and still freezing. It was horrible last night trying to keep warm with no fire. Andy and Jim were shivering so much. We tried to huddle together for body warmth, but with Jim's broken leg, it was hard.

"My friends are hurt bad. I'm scared the bear'll come after them. Do you think it'll take a long while to find them? You could drive me up the highway. Maybe I'll recognize something about where I came out."

"You sit tight. The crew'll take care of it. You're not in such great shape yourself. I'll have Rosie put in a call to the Wilderness Center. Their wildlife rangers may have had reports of a marauding bear. Anyway, we have to report any suspicious animal activity to them. Anything else?"

"No. Not that I can think of. Please hurry. It was so cold. I tried and tried but couldn't get the damn fire started last night. Those guys must be hurting bad."

"Try to calm down, Bob. We'll find them. Our rescue crew's the best. I'm going to get you a cup of hot coffee. Want sugar? Cream? Both?"

Bob nodded. He put his head down into his hands and started to cry softly. Ellie pulled a folding chair over next to him and sat, patting his arm.

"It'll be okay. Don't worry. It's going to work out just fine. Dave's so experienced. He can do anything and so can those mountain rescue fellows. They're the best. Just wait and see."

Bob raised his head and looked at Ellie with tears running down his face. "I'm so sorry, lady. I didn't mean to disrespect you or the cops. For a minute there, I thought everyone in here was out in Booney-ville. You know, not with it. In New Jersey, we're just right next to the city, you know, New York City, the Big Apple."

Ellie answered rather stiffly, "I'm aware that New York City's called the Big Apple. We do get news up here."

"Sorry if I offended you again, but it's busy down my way, police on every corner. Emergency-call phones on each block. Here, nothing. I couldn't even use my cell. Had to drive fifteen minutes to find help. Then I walk in and the cops think I'm a crook and don't even listen to me. I thought I was in the movie *Deliverance*. I'm so glad I was wrong."

Bob lowered his head again. Dave returned with two mugs of hot coffee, both colored with lots of milk and sweetened with two tablespoons of sugar. He had a bag of doughnuts in his hand.

"These are fresh from the Pastry Shop. Bonnie just picked them up. Have a few. They'll give you some energy, Bob."

Ellie and Bob sipped their coffee and munched on doughnuts, while Dave studied the map some more.

"While we're waiting, tell me what brought you down here this morning, Ellie."

"Oh, Dave, I'm so excited. I can't wait to tell you. Actually, I have a couple of things I think you'll be very interested to learn. First, I have some thoughts about that body I found."

Bob jumped and spilled his coffee. "A body? What body? Where did you find it? Was it—was it one of my friends?"

"No, Bob. It wasn't, I'm sure."

"Whew, sorry. I'm all worked up. When you said *body* all I could see was Jim and the way he looked lying in the snow unconscious. I thought maybe you had seen him or something and I didn't know."

"No, Bob, nothing like that. Yesterday, on a walk, I found a body in the woods near my cabin. It couldn't be one of your friends."

"Yeah," said Dave. "I wanted to talk with you about that same thing. I was going to call you this morning."

"I also have some very important information about those criminals you arrested yesterday."

"I'm sure you do. Word sure gets around fast, doesn't it? And you already have a theory, I suppose?"

"Of course I don't know all the details, or what those men you arrested did or said to you. But, I've been thinking about it. And yes, I do have a theory. I think you'll want to hear what I have to say and I think I better tell you as soon as possible. It's really important."

"Let me get Bob settled and then you and I will have a chat, Ellie. Bob, do you have a motel around here?"

"Down in Greenberg, the Chateau Motel. Our stuff's there. We've got one more night reserved. We were going to leave tomorrow."

"I'll give you a choice. I can have someone drop you off at the motel and you can clean up and get some sleep. Or if you prefer, you can wait in the village, at the Inn by the River, until we locate your friends."

"I'd like to stay here, if you can arrange it. I'll go with one of the search teams if you want. I'll do anything. I want to be here when you bring them out."

"Then I'll have Betsy take care of it. No problem. I know it's got to be hard on you. You must be exhausted and that doesn't help. I'd prefer you stay close by. The wildlife rangers might want to talk to you about the bear's behaviors, looks and so forth. And I'm sure your friends are as worried about you as you are about them."

"I just hope they're okay. What if the bear came back? I'm really scared for them. It was so cold…"

Dave intervened. "I know it must have been horrible for you. We can arrange to have a counselor talk with you if you want. But, if there isn't anything else you can think of that would be helpful in finding your friends, then I think you would be more comfortable over at the inn. Clean up, rest, get something to eat. We'll contact you as soon as we hear something."

"Thanks, I appreciate all you're doing for me, for my friends."

"It'll be a while, I'm warning you. It takes some time to get the volunteers together, to find the right place to look, to carry out injured people. But hopefully, we'll get word on their condition long before they actually arrive. Okay?"

Bob stood and reached his hand out toward Dave. Dave shook it and clapped Bob on the back. "Take it easy, man. We'll do all we can. Betsy out there will arrange for someone to drive you to the inn."

"Thanks. I'm sorry for my attitude earlier. Thanks, Ellie. Hope to see you again."

As Bob left the office, Dave sank into his chair and spun toward Ellie. "Now, tell me all about it. Just what have you come up with this time?"

FORTY-NINE

ELLIE STARTED WITH, "First, I've talked with Dude."

"Oh, have you? And what did the tall Dude have to say for himself ?"

"I knew I was right. You figured it out, too."

"Not exactly. Howie and Doc filled me in on the whole rescue story. I won't go into it now 'cause you're sure to hear it many times at the Pastry Shop. So happens, I called Dude, too. Of course, that's my job, isn't it?"

"Dave. I couldn't help it. I thought you were still out on your adventure over at Wilson's Folly so I was just trying to help."

"I warned you about that, haven't I? How many times?"

"More than I care to remember. But listen to what I found out."

"Go on. I know you will anyway. I'm listening."

"Don't sound so bored. I just might have found out something you didn't, you know."

"Based on past experience, I'd bet you're right. Now go on."

"Dude told me he and his brother decided to get rid of the surgeon's dummy instead of storing it for next year, because it smelled so badly. One of the volunteers, Carter, offered to take the dummy to the dump.

"But the dummy never made it to the dump that day, because as you know, it's not open after 6:00 p.m. Dude didn't know anything about what happened after that. He just assumed Carter dumped the dummy. After I told him where I found it, he was frantic. Said he'd call Carter and get back to me."

"Did he?"

"Right away. You won't believe this story. It seems Carter left the dummy in the back of his truck, thinking he'd get rid of it the next day when the dump opened. He drove home. He lives up at the Pine Lodge Farm where all those young people rent cabins and rooms. Then he went to bed.

"He woke up to a scream. Esther, who works the late shift at the nursing home in Greenberg, saw the body in the back of the truck when she came home from work. She was very upset, even after he reassured her it wasn't a dead body, only a dummy. She calmed down only after he agreed to get rid of it right away. So Carter drove to the Cross Road, parked, then carried the dummy into the woods, and dumped it there. That was a few days ago."

"Thanks, Ellie. You solved that mystery. Just so you know, Dude has written a letter to John, and it'll be published in next week's paper, apologizing to the community and offering to pay any expenses incurred by the fire department for the rescue. He's pretty upset about it. He and his brother have worked so hard to ensure the Ghoulog abides by the rules and regulations. He was mortified that you found the dummy and were frightened."

"So, you already knew all about it, then?"

"I did, Ellie. But thanks for your concern and effort. It's always nice to have some backup."

"You're teasing me."

"Just a little. Let's get on with it. You also said you had thoughts about those people we caught up on Wilson's Folly. Tell me about that."

"You've probably figured that out, too. Please don't let me go on and on if you already know. It's a bit embarrassing."

"Okay. Shoot."

"I got thinking about why they would be up there. When I heard they were criminals from Massachusetts, I guessed they might be those men who robbed the Greenberg bank in September and then disappeared with a million dollars. I know they couldn't have been hiding up on the mountain all this time, because Stan would have spotted them. So, they must have gone up yesterday to find someone or something. Bingo. The money. They must have stashed the money up in the hut."

"Hmm. You might have something there. You're right about who they are. Turns out, they probably are the ones who robbed the bank, although one man from the original bunch wasn't with them. He's still missing. So, you think they were going after the money, huh? Makes sense. Maybe one of the robbers took the money, disguised himself as a hunter, climbed that trail and hid it."

"You're going to check it out, aren't you?"

"Yep."

"Well, when? How?"

"Snow's melting fast. I've contacted Stan and he's searching the hut as we speak."

"Oh, you guessed the money might be there, too."

"Figured it out, just like you. Of course, I had help. Colby and Rosie are a pair of smart officers. They heard the robbers arguing about the money and where it might be hidden. They're the ones who came up with the theory the robbers stashed the money in the hut. You deduced it all by yourself."

"With a little help from Sarah. The money has to be in the hut because there aren't any caves on that trail big enough to hide a bag of money. I read all about the trail in the AMC guidebook. They wouldn't leave a duffel bag of money on the ground or buried because of snow, animals or rain. But no one has figured out where in the hut it's stashed yet, right?"

"Right. Stan's been looking for a couple of hours with no luck. He thinks we must be wrong. There just aren't that many places to hide anything in that little hut, certainly not a duffel bag of money."

"Maybe I can help you after all," Ellie said.

"How?"

"I think I know where they hid it."

FIFTY

"WHERE?" DAVE ASKED, awe in his voice.

"Let me backtrack a bit. First, I've watched the bank's security tape very closely. I believe one of the robbers worked in the bank."

"Yeah, why? The FBI has been interrogating the staff at the bank for months. They're all suspects, but nothing has come up that points to anyone conclusively."

"Two reasons, Dave. First, the FBI doesn't know the local people like we do. If they did they would have figured out Henry Beson, the bank's senior loan officer, was the sixth robber."

"Beson? How'd you single him out?"

"Simple, once I put my mind and my computer to it. Only two men work in the bank front offices, Henry Beson and Jacob Swan. Jacob's an older man, walks with a limp, churchgoing type, with a rich wife. Henry Beson's younger and word has it he spends a lot of time at the casino gambling. So unless the sixth robber was a woman, it had to be Beson."

"Hmm," Dave mumbled. "You found this out on the computer?"

"I found out two ways. I knew one robber had to be a man and probably worked in the bank because I saw his shoes. I didn't put it all together until this morning.

"Last night I dreamed about the robbery again. I was lying on the cold floor, scared to death. Some of the robbers walked by me. All I could see was their shoes. I saw three sets. Two were black sneakers, like all the other robbers wore. The third set were brown loafers, shiny polished work-type shoes. I've been trying to remember that fact for months. It almost drove me crazy."

"Wow. That's astonishing. I knew you were blocked on some facts and were working to remember them. So last night you dreamed of the shoes. That's wild."

"When I woke up and realized I had remembered the shoes, I felt so relieved. It's been a load on my mind for a long time. In all the excitement of yesterday, I forgot about the robbery. And last night, I remembered. James told me it could happen that way and it did."

"Boy, are we lucky to have you on our side. You'd be tough to beat if you were on the other side."

"Want me to go on?"

"Certainly. Let's have it all."

"Well, the other reason I had suspected Beson was what I found out when I Googled him."

"You what?"

"Googled him. You know, looked him up on the Internet. I found out he was on the list of delinquent tax-payers. That's public information. Now why didn't he pay his taxes?"

"Because he didn't have the money?"

"Right. A single man like him, a senior loan officer, makes enough money to pay his real estate taxes, unless he has other outstanding debts. My guess is he owed money to pay off his gambling debt and the loan sharks called in the loan. When he couldn't pay, the mob moved in. They must have forced him to rob the bank to pay his debt, or die."

"Hmm," Dave scribbled a note on his desk blotter. "I'm with you so far. Beson agrees to the robbery to get off the hook. The crooks get the information about the Brink's delivery from him and make him take part, so he's implicated in the crime and won't rat them out. He's right in the office, so just slips on the black sweats and ski mask in his office and joins the robbers when they come in. But he forgets to change his shoes. Then afterward, he doesn't get in the van with them. He's the sixth man, the one missing in the tape when the others escape."

Ellie rubbed her chin and thought. "I think he runs back in the bank. His body would be blocked by the other robbers if he bent down and walked behind them in the other direction. Back into the bank.

"The robbers had warned everyone to stay down. So he sneaks in his office, strips off the disguise and lays down on the floor, with the rest of us. Gets up when the ten minutes are up and acts like he was a victim, too."

"But what about the money? If I remember correctly, the duffel bag of money wasn't visible in the last sighting, when the robbers got into the van."

"Right. I think Beson carried it into his office. He hid it there until the police were through with their investigation. Somehow he got it out of the bank, probably after hours or he came back at night to get it. He has a key. Maybe he came in early and stashed it in his car before anyone else was there."

"Wouldn't the camera pick him up?"

"Sure, but he might have hidden the money in something. Maybe he pretended he came in early to clean out his office and packed the money in a bin under some personal stuff. Or maybe he took it out in his clothes, a little at a time."

"Okay. I'll go along with you. The FBI could certainly check the tapes days after the robbery and see if Beson was carrying anything out. Then what do you think Beson did?"

"I figured that out when I Googled him. Did you know he's a mountain guide in his spare time? And get this, his specialty's the Wilson Folly trail. He even has a Web site showing the views from the trail, the hut, and advertising what he provides for lunch on the way up."

"So?"

"So he's gone up and down that trail a lot. In addition, on his Web site he shows photos of the inside of the hut. Funny thing, he seems to show a lot of pictures of the fireplace, especially the stone hearth. Maybe it was his way of documenting where he hid the money if anything happened to him."

"The money's under the hearth?"

"I'd bet on it. I also Googled the State Mountain Park site and guess what I found."

"Tell me. I'm all ears."

"The blueprints for the hut. In the archives are blueprints of all the buildings built in the last decade. The blueprints for the Wilson Hut show a space under the left side of the hearth. A space big enough for a large duffel bag."

"Wow. How'd the space get there? Usually hearths are pretty sturdy. They've got to hold a lot of weight, the chimney bricks, etcetera."

"Yes, but this hearth had to be positioned on a slab of ledge and the ledge falls off on the left side, leaving a large space. All Beson had to do was lift the flagstone on that side and push in the duffel bag."

"I'm calling Stan now. Stay right there."

Dave called Stan, told him about Beson, and asked him to look for the loose flagstone. He'd hold. A minute later Stan picked up the phone and said, "Dave, you're remarkable. I've been in charge of this hut for two years and I've never noticed that loose stone. I pulled out the duffel bag and it's full of money, big bills. Beson must have put it here, but they can check for prints and fibers. I put on gloves, but maybe Beson didn't. He guided hikers up here almost every weekend. Sometimes he hiked up alone and stayed overnight. He's been here when I'm checking out another part of the park, so he could have easily come up here alone, hid the duffel, and hiked down without me ever knowing he was here."

"Don't tell me I'm remarkable. Ellie Hastings's sitting right here with me. She's the one who figured it all out. As usual, she's the master sleuth. I'll tell you about it later. For now, secure that duffel. I'm calling Jenkins at the FBI office in Greenberg and telling him where the money is and how we think it got there. Thanks, Stan. I'll be back in touch."

Dave hung up the phone and smiled at Ellie, who was leaning back in her chair with a sweet smile of triumph on her face.

"I think we should call you Miss Hastings or Sherlock Hastings from now on. You're really something. Maybe even better than your Miss Marple. Way to go, Ellie."

Ellie demurely stated, "It was nothing, Dave. Anybody who wasn't too busy could have done the same thing. But thank you anyway. I'm glad I could help."

FIFTY-ONE

CAW, CAW, CAW. The repeated calling of crows woke Ellie out of a deep sleep. Darkness surrounded her. She turned over and reached for the clock by the side of her bed. It wasn't there. She stretched her hand out farther. No clock, no lamp, and where were her glasses?

By now, Ellie was wide-awake, wondering what was going on. She could hear Buddy snoring softly. His head was on her lap. But she wasn't in her bed.

Then she remembered. After the events of the previous day, Rosie had driven Ellie and Buddy back home in style, perched in the Hummingbird Falls big black SUV. Dusk had been falling by then. To avoid getting snowy slush all over the pine floors, they had waved goodbye to Rosie and tromped around the cabin to the back door. Ellie had set the pie box down on the step while she opened the door. Then she had put her overnight case inside and stood aside so Buddy could go in. Exhausted, she had shut the door and removed her boots and coat, leaving the overnight case where it was.

Ellie had thrown some kindling and logs into the wood stove and got a good hot fire going. That effort had stolen the last of her strength. She and Buddy had lain down on the couch in front of the warm fire in the living room and were soon asleep. That is, until the crows startled Ellie awake.

She hadn't turned the lights on when she came home and must have slept for hours. The wood stove was almost out. She'd have to fill it again.

Then she thought, Why are the crows cawing at night?

That was strange. From her research on crows, she learned they were usually quiet at night to avoid detection by night predators, such as owls. She had heard crows making a fuss at night only once before. At the cottage she had rented, the place where Millie, Todd and their three kids lived now, crows had woken her in the middle of the night, like tonight. The next morning she found animal tracks circling her house. Mike told her they were coyote tracks and sometimes a hungry coyote would stalk a house for dog food dishes left out, a pet chained in the yard or trash cans not properly closed. He informed her that crows would voice their warnings about intruders mostly during daylight hours, but occasionally at night, too.

So, what were the crows trying to warn her about? She peered out the windows but saw only the star-studded sky and the whiteness of the remaining snow-drifts against the dark silhouette of the forest. And Buddy continued to sleep, snoring in little soft grunts. Therefore, whatever the crows were cautioning about wasn't human. Buddy always barked when humans approached.

As she built up the fire, she recalled the afternoon's events. She had kept Bob company at the Inn by the River while they waited for the rescuers to report. Wildlife specialists arrived and interviewed Bob about the bear, which had attacked the hunters. They asked for a description, details about its behavior toward the men, and how the hunters reacted. Bob could tell them very little, other than how frightened they were. It was dark, they were in shock, and the scene too chaotic to describe.

The wildlife rangers assured Bob they would be hunting for the bear. If they caught it, they would need to study the animal and analyze the situation to determine what steps to take next. It could be released in another county, put to sleep, or confined. From the story Bob told them, they were not convinced this was a rogue or killer bear. Nobody else had reported an aggressive black bear this season. They suspected this one was hungry and when shot, tried to escape, hurting the men in his attempt to flee. They did not believe it had maliciously attacked the hunters. However, the outcome would not be determined until they found it.

A few hours later Dave called Bob and informed him the rescuers had located both lost hunters. They were alive and rescue crews were in the process of airlifting both Andy and Jim by helicopter and flying them to the Greenberg Memorial Hospital. Later, Dave picked Ellie and Bob up and drove to the hospital, where they learned both men would survive their injuries and hypothermia. They would need surgery, then recovery time, but should be okay. After Dave briefly interviewed the men, he left Bob to oversee their treatment and he and Ellie returned to Hummingbird Falls's police station.

When they arrived, Betsy had two big news items for them. The man Rosie found shot on the trail was officially identified as Henry Beson, the loan officer at the

Greenberg Federal Bank. The bullet found in his head matched one of the guns Dave had taken from the group arrested on Wilson's trail.

Ironically, the sixth robber turned up when Colby found and stopped the man in the Massachusetts car who had earlier picked up Bob on the highway and dropped him off at the police station.

The sixth robber had decided it was too dangerous for him to join his fellow thieves climbing the trail. He stayed at his motel room watching TV and waiting for the others to return. When they didn't show up in person, but instead were featured on the late news for being arrested and charged with robbing the Greenberg Federal Bank, he prepared to leave for Boston early the next morning.

When Colby pulled him over and tried to explain he needed him to return to the police station to help out the rescuers, the man became angry and suspicious. Colby asked for his license and registration. The man responded by starting his car and racing off. Colby followed him in a high-speed chase, finally forcing him to the side of the highway. Colby handcuffed him and brought him back to the Hummingbird Falls police station.

The man turned out to be the top boss, Jimmy Cardino, a well-known mobster from Boston. Dave and Colby took Cardino to the Greenberg jail where the district attorney would arraign him and the rest of his gang. Rosie had volunteered to take Ellie and Buddy home.

It had been a long, but interesting and exciting day. No wonder she and Buddy were exhausted.

When Ellie had the fire going, she turned on the lights and busied herself washing up the dirty dishes and wiping off the counters. Then she changed into her soft flannel pajamas and prepared to go to bed.

Suddenly, she realized that her head didn't hurt as much as it had. The pain had diminished throughout the day. Thank goodness. Tomorrow she could get back to the poem she was going to write. And what else? Oh, of course, get back on her diet. She had shamefully eaten two blueberry turnovers yesterday and doughnuts today. No more. She was determined this time to follow through on a new and healthier life style.

Ellie walked into the living room and woke Buddy up. He jumped off the couch, took a couple of sips of water, walked into the bedroom, jumped up on Ellie's bed and immediately fell asleep again.

"Well, you deserve it, you good dog. You saved my life. No wonder you're tired, having to drag me all the way home in a blizzard. Sleep well."

FIFTY-TWO

ELLIE WOKE EARLY the next morning. She smiled as she realized her head did not hurt at all. The bump on the back of her head had reduced to a small sore spot and the cut on her temple had scabbed over and no longer hurt even if she pressed on it.

The sun was pouring through her windows illuminating the floating dust motes. Ellie grimaced.

"Better do some dusting and vacuuming, Buddy."

Buddy got right up when he heard the word, vacuum, the most dreaded word in his life. He hated the vacuum cleaner. His nemesis howled, sucked, chased him around the house and drove him mad. His food and water dishes disappeared. His bones and toys were picked up and unavailable. No matter where he tried to hide, the vacuum found him. He moved from one room to the next and stayed alert, listening for the growling creature, waiting for it to search him out once again. He whined at Ellie.

"Okay, Buddy. I know you hate when I vacuum. But we'll get dressed, eat our breakfast and go out for a little while before I start. It looks beautiful outside. I think the snow will be gone soon with this bright warm sun."

After breakfast, Ellie and Buddy started out to the backyard to fill the bird feeders and play ball. As soon as she opened the door, she knew something was wrong. A purple-blue mess covered the steps and something big had left large paw marks everywhere.

"Oh, Buddy. The blueberry pie I bought for Sarah. I left it on the back steps last night. I totally forgot about it. That's why those crows were making so much noise last night. Something came and got the pie."

Ellie spotted the pie tin and Pastry Shop box ripped open under the bird feeders. The snow there was bluish-purple, too, and all messed up. She followed the trail of prints with her eyes. They led to the brush at the back of the yard.

"Too big for a squirrel. Might be a raccoon, but he'd have to be really huge. Maybe it was a coyote? What do you think, Buddy?"

Buddy was too busy sniffing the tracks to think. The smell tantalized him and bothered him as well. His hair began to rise up like porcupine quills. His nose traveled from one track to the next, thoroughly investigating each paw mark. He looked up at Ellie and barked. Then he followed the tracks, one by one.

Ellie watched the edge of the yard as she picked up the ripped-open pie box and tin. The family of crows was sitting in the top of the tallest pine, watching her. The crows didn't seem worried about a scavenger being close, so she relaxed. They'd be screaming murder like last night if some big critter were still around.

She went to the shed and got the garden shovel. She wanted to get rid of the messy blueberries that covered her back steps. She trudged back to the steps and started shoveling up the gooey shambles of all that remained of a blueberry piecrust and filling.

Buddy started barking wildly. The crows broke into a hideous chorus of frightening calls. Buddy ran to

Ellie's side with his tail between his legs. Ellie looked up and saw the crows in flight. They circled in the air over her, cawing raucously. As she watched, the crows dipped down in a group and dove toward the back bushes as if they were missiles tracking a target. They swerved at the last minute and flew up into the air again. They started to circle the backyard, still crying out their piercing warnings.

Then she saw the bear.

FIFTY-THREE

THE BEAR LOOKED RIGHT at her. Then he started to walk toward her and Buddy, across the gardens, across the lawn, under the bird feeders. Closer and closer.

Saving Buddy was the only thing on Ellie's mind as she watched the big bear limp slowly across the yard. She could hear Buddy's deep-throated growl behind her legs, where she had pushed him as soon as she saw the huge bear coming toward them. Buddy struggled to get out of her hold. He wanted to move in front of her, but she held on to his collar and kept him back. If he got loose…she couldn't finish the thought. The bear might attack if it saw the dog and got defensive. What should she do?

She couldn't call anyone. Her cell phone was inside. She didn't dare turn her back on the bear, he might rush her. She couldn't reach the door in time to let Buddy and herself inside. So she did the only thing she could think of.

She squeezed Buddy tightly between her legs so he couldn't move. That freed her other hand. Then with both hands, she raised the shovel high into in the air. Maybe the bear would think would think she was bigger than she was.

As the bear came slowly closer, she could see it was injured. Blood had crusted on its back and side and it was limping badly.

The bear didn't act as she expected. She had antici-
pated a wild attack, the bear standing up over her, ready
to bite and slash her to pieces. But this bear just walked,
watching her, swinging his huge head side to side, and
whining softly. She noticed it was thin and seemed
sick. She hesitated.

The bear stopped walking and merely stood there,
staring at her. Maybe it needed her help. Was that why
it was coming to her this way? Maybe she should try
to help it. But how? She didn't know anything about
bears except she was frightened of them.

A thought struck her. It might have rabies. That
would account for its thin, sick condition and for its
odd, out-of-character behavior. She couldn't let it get
near Buddy. If it had rabies, it would pass the disease
with one nip, one bite.

The bear took a few steps closer. He stopped again,
looked back toward the woods. The crows wheeling
overhead took this opportunity and dove for him again.
One crow managed to claw the bear's back while
another pecked at his head in passing. Too late, the
bear tried to lift his paw and swipe at them. By then they
were too high and out of danger.

The bear turned back to Ellie. Buddy wiggled to
free himself. The dog's action agitated the bear. He
lifted his head, growled at Buddy, and started to move
closer, his drooling mouth open, looking ready to bite.

When the bear was so close Ellie could smell it, see
the yellow on its teeth, and hear its heavy breathing, she
made her move. She jumped off the porch stair and
slammed the heavy steel shovel on the bear's head with
all the force she could muster. Then she grabbed Buddy,
turned and ran for the door.

She got to the door, expecting to feel claws rip down her back. She pulled the door open, pushed Buddy inside, anticipating excruciating pain on her legs, her head.

Then she was through the door. She locked it and looked out the window. The bear lay still on the path. It didn't move. Ellie couldn't see any steaming breath coming from its open mouth.

She ran for her cell phone and dialed Sarah's number while she cautiously opened the back door and stepped out, leaving Buddy inside.

When Sarah answered, Ellie whispered very quietly, "Hello, Sarah. It's me."

"Ellie, is that you? Ellie? Why aren't you talking louder? Are you okay?"

Ellie whispered again. "Sorry, I'm afraid to talk louder. Try to listen harder."

"Ellie, if you don't speak up and answer me right now I'm going to call the police dispatcher and have her send Dave out there. It's 7:00 a.m. You called me. Now say something."

"I'm not okay. I killed him. He's dead and I did it," Ellie said a little louder.

"You what? Killed who?"

"Not who, Sarah, it."

"But you said you killed *him.* Did you kill an *it,* too? Who is *it?*"

"*It* isn't a who. It's an *it,* a *what.*"

"Ellie, you're not making sense. You said you killed *him,* then *it,* now *it's* a *what.* I'm totally confused. Just what did you do?"

"I killed a bear."

"A bear? You? Come on. You've got to be kidding."

"I'm not kidding. I really killed it. It's lying on the ground next to my back porch, not moving. I'm looking at him right now."

"Be careful. Are you sure he's—*it's*—dead?"

"Pretty sure. It's not moving a muscle."

"How did you kill it?"

"I hit him with my garden shovel."

"Oh, my God. With your shovel? But why?"

"It was coming toward me. I thought it might have rabies. I was scared Buddy would get rabies from him. I just wanted to stop it."

"Buddy? What about you?"

"I didn't think about that."

"So you walked over and whacked him on the head? Weren't you scared?"

"I was so scared for Buddy, I lost it. It didn't matter if it was a bear or a vampire. Anything that threatens Buddy has got to go through me first."

"Tell me everything."

"Well, when it got close enough I jumped off the porch stair and whanged him over the head. Now I feel just awful. I didn't mean to kill him. I didn't want him dead, just stopped. Oh, Sarah, he looked so pathetic, old and sick. I think he must have been shot or something because he was limping and bleeding. I didn't know what to do. I didn't want to hurt him, just to stop him from getting Buddy. I'm so sorry." Ellie started sobbing.

"What are you going to do now?"

"I don't know. That's why I called you. You're a United States Postmistress, aren't you? Doesn't the government have rules about what to do when you kill a bear? I don't know if it's even bear hunting season."

"Ellie, you must be really upset to say a stupid thing

like that. Bear rules come from the State Forestry and Wildlife Department. I don't know what the hunting rules are. I may deal in wildlife stamps, but that's as close as I am to bear information."

"But I don't know anyone in the Forestry Department. You're the closest one to government I could come up with."

"What does it matter anyhow? He—*it*—was attacking you, wasn't he? Nobody will care about the rules."

There was no reply.

"Ellie? Ellie? Say something."

Sarah didn't hear anything.

"Ellie, you're breaking up. Are you on your cell?"

"Yes. I'm just off the porch on the walk, watching the bear."

"Well, go back inside. It's cold out there, isn't it?"

"I didn't notice, but now that you mention it, yes. Oh. Oh, my gosh. Oh, dear."

"What is it? What's happening? Talk to me. I can't hear you. What?"

"Sarah, forget it. Forget everything I said."

"What? The reception's awful. It sounds like you're huffing and puffing."

"I was wrong. I didn't kill the bear after all. He's up and running after me. I'm running back to the house. He's coming closer. He's coming up the stairs."

"Ellie, Ellie. I can't hear you. Ellie…damn. Did we get disconnected? Ellie, where are you? Why aren't you talking? Are you okay? Ellie, if you don't answer me right now I'm going to call Dave. Say something. Ellie, hold on. I'm calling Dave and the Wildlife Rangers."

FIFTY-FOUR

THE SNOW BEGAN TO FALL. Large white flakes floated down. The crowd began to break up and move slowly away to their cars and trucks. Some people wiped their eyes as they passed the black box, lying in the open, speckled with white flakes.

"Who would have ever guessed something like this would happen?" Mary asked Dave as they started to walk down the long driveway to where they had parked their car.

"I hope the frosted brownies I left help a little. It's so hard to know what to do when something like this happens."

"I know," said Dave. "What a terrible thing. I hope I never have to go through something like this again."

Colby and Rosie joined them. "How're you doing, boss?" Colby asked.

Dave turned. "I want to thank you both for all you did. I don't know what would have happened if you hadn't been so quick getting here."

Rosie answered, "We put the pedal to the metal, all right. This man can really drive. I thought the Wildlife Rangers were going to faint when we ripped around the U-turn on the Winding Hill Road."

Mary looked sharply at Rosie.

"Sorry, I didn't mean to sound disrespectable, Mary."

"No, it's all right. I wouldn't have minded seeing that for myself, that's all I meant. Must have been pretty funny."

They all started to laugh.

"Wait up, will you?"

Ellie's voice and Buddy's bark turned them around.

"Ellie. We thought you might be ready for a little peace and quiet, after all this," said Dave.

"Well, actually, I'm feeling quite a bit better now that the veterinarian said Old Scar Face would survive. I was so afraid I'd killed him."

"You must have been surprised when he came back to life," said Rosie.

"I don't think *surprised* is quite the right word," Ellie answered. "I just dropped the phone outside and ran. That bear must have been really woozy because he just lay back down and went to sleep on top of my cell phone. I'm sorry I scared everyone."

"Some thought you might be bear dinner," Colby added. "Although those of us who know you thought it more likely you'd be cooking up bear stew."

"How can you say such a thing? I love animals. I hate eating them. I'm thinking about becoming a vegetarian."

A big truck rolled up the driveway, carrying a winch.

"I guess they're ready to load him up now," Ellie said. "Those Wildlife Rangers are really something. Albert hit him with the dart, first thing. After that, no one had to worry. They dragged him into the bear cage and I think he's still asleep."

"They'll take good care of him, don't worry," Dave said. "The vet told me he'd need some surgery for the bullet wounds, lots of food and rest, but should be ready to return to the wild in a week or so. If they feed him up good, he should go straight into hibernation and be no worse for the wear, come next spring."

"Where are they taking him?" Ellie asked.

Colby said, "First to the animal hospital and then up to the Wildlife Preserve in Davidson County. No hunting's allowed up there and there's plenty of food available. He might outlive us all."

"I was happy they assessed him as a healthy bear, and not dangerous," Mary said. "From what I heard, he was just really hungry and trying to fatten up to survive the winter. Those hunters got in his way. They were ignorant and didn't follow the rules of the wild. They have no one to blame but themselves."

"They're lucky to be alive. By the way, Bob's left to go back to New Jersey. He's a nice guy. He said his friends should be out of the hospital in a week. They don't plan on hunting again real soon." Dave laughed.

"They'll be out of the hospital before the bad guys from Massachusetts even get to court," said Colby. "The way their lawyer is playing with extradition and a lot of jumbled-up complaints, they may not ever get to court."

Rosie nodded. "Then, they better not ever show up around here again. I've got some bruises I owe them."

Dave said, "I don't think you have to worry. They'll get what they deserve. It happens that way most of the time."

Everyone nodded.

"And hunting season'll be over pretty soon. Peace will return to the mountains and valleys. I can't wait," Ellie said.

"Peace?" Dave queried. "Before you know it, Ellie, you'll be trying to solve something else. People are learning that you're the one to come to if there's a mystery to be solved. After all those news stories about the Ghoulog, the bank robbers and the bear, your reputation's nationwide. You'll be getting a slue of calls, I bet."

"Well, Dude and his brother did ask me to work with them on the Ghoulog's haunting story for next year's show. But so far, that's the only request I've had. Thank goodness. I have pictures to paint, poems to write, children and a grandchild to visit, seed catalogs to study, friends to see. Too much to do to get into any more mysteries. And, if Buddy and I can just get through winter, then I'll officially be a year-round citizen of Hummingbird Falls."

James walked up as Ellie finished talking. "That's a good reason to celebrate, then. Let's all go down to O'Callahan's and have pizza together."

To a chorus of cheers, James put his arm around Ellie and took Buddy's leash from her. They started down the driveway. The rumble of the big truck stopped them and they stepped back as the truck passed, carrying the big black bear house with the sleeping Old Scar Face inside.

After a moment of silence, James continued, "After dinner, we can come back and devour Mary's frosted brownies."

Another cheer rose as the six Hummingbird Falls residents walked down the driveway, catching snow-flakes in their hair and on their eyelashes. Ellie turned her head up, smiling, and watched the flakes fall. She caught sight of the seven crows frolicking in the red pine treetop. She sent a silent thank-you to them. Then she opened her mouth and caught a few snowflakes. "Yum," she said.

ELLIE'S POEM

Changes

Frost stole in and killed my blooms
Leaving me with dirt and gloom.
I wasn't ready for the change.
Life is different, all rearranged.
I live on faith that time will mend
The pain the empty spot still sends.

I trust that order has its way.
That change will happen come what may.
And so I am not too surprised
When daffodils begin to rise
And crocus fill the empty spot.
I like this new change quite a lot.